Homecoming

THE SEQUEL TO "LATE REGISTRATION"

SHERIDAN S. DAVIS

CHOCOLATE CHIP & CO. PUBLISHING

To those of us who have been ticked off by love and everything that looks like it, may it all come together in time.

Dear Reader...

I'm so sorry it took me this long to complete this story. Life has been happening a bit harder than I anticipated. Regardless, you all are my family and my priority. If you haven't, subscribe to my YouTube channel for updates and free content. Please, share this book with literally everyone, as it is a labor of love.

Now, this book has a lot of cursing and some sexually explicit content. If you don't wish to read this kind of material, please, check out some of my other work! If you have not read "Late Registration," close this book and start there.

God bless you,
Sheridan S. Davis

Soundtrack

WARNING, listening while reading can have you DEEP in your feelings.

Come Through - H.E.R. ft. Chris Brown
Backin' It Up - Pardison Fontaine ft. Cardi B.
It's Alright - Chanté Moore
Forever Don't Last - Jazmine Sullivan
Selfish - PnB Rock
Bad N Boujee - Migos
Mask Off - Future
Damage - Amg Manson
Distance - Yebba
Pressure - Ari Lennox
You Are My High - DJ Snake
Shepherd - Cece Winans

Alabaster Box - Cece Winans

All Yours Violet Tyson

Midnight Snack - Muni Long ft. Jacob Latimore

Plastic Off The Sofa - Beyoncé

Every Kind of Way - H.E.R.

I woke up on top of my newly subscribed boyfriend. He didn't have to give me a wake-up call this morning. My soul had been awake since last night. I blinked, or at least I tried to. Eye boogers had formed in the corners of my lids, paralyzing them. I knew I looked a mess. I felt groggy, too. But along with that groggy feeling, was that of a champion. I gave the man some cuddy last night. Twice. And as hard as he was snoring in my ears, I think he liked it. I did, too, after a while. I could feel dampness and soreness down there, and I knew I needed to go take care of it. I pushed up to go soak in his tub, but as soon as I did, I was met with resistance. Chance's arms held me close to him as he stirred in his sleep.

"Where you going?" he groaned with me in his arms. His breath smelled of me and sleep. Not caring about that though, he brought me in for a kiss. We pushed past the staleness and enjoyed one another. I could feel his enjoyment a little too much.

"Mmm mmm..." I denied him. "I got to pee," I sang out.

"Grr..." He growled and flipped me on my back. "No, you don't. You're running." He kissed my neck and started moving downward.

"Broderick, I'm sore," I wined. I was carrying on like a baby, knowing I wanted him to pamper me.

"Let daddy take care of you," he spoke into my microphone.

"Booooy, you gon' make a hoe out of me," I sang and prepared for lift-off.

Chance had me for breakfast, per usual, but I was hungry for real food. After each of us showered, we decided to go to The Golden Nugget to eat. We went down the elevator hand-in-hand, as if we didn't have a care in the world—because we didn't. I would deal with the consequences later, but I was loving him in this moment. We crossed the street to the parking lot and stood in awe at the sight of his car.

"I know I'm halluci-damn-nating right now!" Chance screamed and walked around his car in a circle. "I know this ain't my shit!"

"Oh my God!" I gasped.

"Yo', here's my credit cards," he handed me his wallet. "You gon' have to bail me out 'cause I'm going the hell to prison, b! WHO DID THIS?!" He was barking and howling something serious, and I understood every second of it.

"Baby, you got to try to calm—"

"You call yourself a Brother?" we heard from behind. I knew that voice backwards and forward. When we turned around, we saw Zaïre standing adjacent to a nearby vehicle with The Brothers standing beside him. He must've just come from football practice because he was donning his uniform. Noticeably missing from the crew was Romeo.

"This you?" Chance pointed to the damage on his car that was clearly done at the hands of the Omegas. Syrup—what looked to be gallons of it—had been poured all over Chance's car. Windows, doors, hood, trunk, exhaust pipe. They were all drenched in the breakfast condiment.

Zaïre pointed in my direction and said, "That's me. And you're in straight violation right now, Frat!"

My mouth flew open! Was this happening right now? In real life? I was beyond stunned. Never had I ever thought Zaïre would be bold enough to pull something like this. Chance's face screwed up. "I ain't violate shit!" His hands balled into fists.

"I got word that you been eating my leftovers. And you told her about Taylor? That's treason, my boy! A violation! You ain't think you would have to see me about that, bruh?"

Zaïre inched up closer to Chance. He got word? I pieced together everything he was saying. Chance walked up in Zaïre's face and tapped him on the temple. "I ain't tell her shit! But if I had, I'm trying to figure out what you was gon' do about it, nigga?"

His teeth were clinched, but I heard every word. My stomach churned where I stood, listening to this back and forth. "You ain't man enough to rock the letters. You ain't brother enough for Omega. You's a backstabbing nigga. I hope you enjoyed my sidepiece, mark. When you kiss her, tell me how my ass taste. Disrespectfully, nigga," Zaïre challenged him. This war—ego and pride—was too much. I was being lied on and disrespected to my face. I'd had enough.

"What the hell did you just say?" I screamed. Zy turned to me with angry eyes. He had to have forgotten I was even there because him throwing out false sexual allegations concerning me would never be the move.

"Zaïre, I will beat your ass! Don't insinuate nothing about me! I already owe you one for finding that girl in your room! Don't be out here saying no 'Tell me how my ass taste' bull crap! You ain't Big Shaq, nigga!"

"Skylar, let me handle it!" Chance cut in.

"Don't Skylar me!" I yelled at him. "Zaïre, you will not try to make me look like a hoe. I was a virgin the whole time I was with you! I ain't ever ate your nasty ass, though you begged me to eat mine! Don't go there with me!"

"Real talk, you's a straight up pass around! You going from me to my frat? A nigga ain't gon' turn down no coochie so I'm madder at your deceiving ass than him! And I'm glad your friend told me the shit you was doing behind my back! You wanted to make me feel bad for Taylor...whole time you been fucking my frat, but was begging me to wait on your ass? You a bird!" Zaïre lamented.

"I will..." Chance started running towards Zaïre in an aggressive manner. I was glad he hadn't pulled out his gun. A crowd of people had begun to circle around us.

"Nah, you a bird!" I yelled at the top of my lungs. "I ain't violate with Chance, but I could have! I don't give a shit what Sage told you! You had me couped up in some dorm while your dusty ass was out here parading this girl around in the streets and you got the nerve to say I was cheating?

"You frontin' for these niggas!" I continued ballistically, while ten Brothers tried holding Chance back. He was having a shoving match with one of them. They were so preoccupied with him that they didn't see me coming up on Zaïre. I ran to him, screaming like a mad woman, while Chance circled behind me. "You too broke to be out here cheating, my boy!"

Zaïre's eyes doubled in size. I was beside myself with anger, using cuss words that I'd sworn off.

"Your ego got me fucked up! You had me sneaking out my parents' house to bring food to your hungry ass on Christmas; you convinced me to come to this school, and this is how you do me? With your raggedy ass?"

"Shut the—" "You finish that sentence, and I was zap your ass into the next decade, Zaïre!" I gripped my purse with my stun gun in it. He knew I was holding. "With your welfare ass! Who bought that syrup? Because I know it wasn't you! You calling me a hoe because you're embarrassed, but you don't compare to Chance on any level! Not one! Mentally, physically, financially, or sexually, nigga! Now while you're worried about my vagina, you need to be worried about your feet! Run me them cleats up off your feet since you like to call women hoes, hoe! Did you tell these niggas I bought them?"

"Skylar," one of the Brothers tried to calm me down.

"Don't call my name! You ain't try to save me from embarrassment when this nigga was calling me all kinds of birds and hoes, lying on me!" I yelled. Then, I recalled the cards someone had been sliding underneath my door. It was him. It was all him. "Bend down and take them off!" I yelled. "Make it to the NFL barefooted with ya hoe ass!"

Zaïre had tears in his eyes, he was so embarrassed. I had fire in mine. He toed out of the shoes while standing erect. He kicked the left one off, and it hit my shin; that's when all hell broke loose. Chance broke free and punched the hell out of Zy, sending him cascading to the ground.

"Stop!" I yelled. I didn't need Chance going to jail or getting kicked out of school for trying to defend my honor—not right now. I stood in front of him, trying to keep up with every move he made as his feet danced around Zaïre, who'd gotten back up. "You my frat!"

Chance yelled. "I'm KOP until I'm DOA, but don't ever disrespect my wife!"

"Your wife?" Zaïre stretched his riddled chin. "She was my girl!"

"Nah, Taylor was!" Chance objected.

"Both of you, just shut up!" I released Chance and turned to face Zy. I picked up the cleats from the ground as tears began welling in my eyes. "Y'all egos and this toxic fucking masculinity are too damn much to take! You cavemen assholes! Zaïre, don't say shit else to me! And don't slide another note up under my door. The next time you do it, it ain't gon' be no talking!" I began limping away, having enough of their vibrato. "Oh," I turned back to face Zy. "And my brother will be at this school to see yo' ass, nigga!" And with that, I walked off, squeezing my way through the crowd to get back upstairs. I walked into the Angelous with my right hand gripping my stomach, and my left hand carrying cleats.

I was more than embarrassed; I was vexed and humiliated. I knew people would find out we were together one day, but I hadn't fathomed all this. I mowed over the words that were exchanged between the two guys, while blocking everything else out. I was caught in the middle of a war of two Titans—two Black soldiers. I was their Helen of Troy. One of the soldiers had been the suitor of my youth while the other met the needs of my womanhood. A trojan war had broken out and I was caught in the middle. It was a sword fight. Although I had been the catalyst, I also became a casualty in their game of bravado. When the elevator opened, I stepped inside with tears streaming down my face. I was hurt by both suitors, stabbed by their words, and gut-punched by the reality. Before the elevator doors could close, Chance ran inside. He tried to hug me, but I pushed him away with my left hand—the hand with the cleats.

"Baby," he started, but I put my hand up to halt his sentence.

"You knew this whole time?"

He'd known about Taylor. He saw me crying over her and Zaïre's relationship. He knew about her yet never said a word.

"Listen..."

"No, you listen. Before we got together, you were my friend. My best friend. You knew and didn't tell me?" I was shocked. And hurt.

"I didn't know you at first. And that's my frat so I just didn't say anything, babe. But after I got know you, and we became close, it was about not hurting you. I didn't want to be the bearer of that info. I'm sorry. I swear I am." He pleaded. I looked up at the numbers on the elevator, waiting for them to get to my floor. "Baby," Chance was in my face in seconds, grabbing my chin, trying to make me look at him.

"I don't want to talk!" I yelled. "I can be your sounding board, but you have information about my life and don't say anything?" I scoffed. The elevator doors opened. I took a step to get off, but he blocked my path to get through the doors. "Move, Chance!" I screamed.

"Chance?" he sounded wounded by the mention of his own middle name. "I ain't Chance to you, baby. I'm Broderick. I didn't want to be the one to bring you that shit. I didn't want to hurt you. I didn't want to see the look you have on your face right now. I was trying to protect you from the truth."

"Some protection," I scoffed.

"You're a liar!"

"I'm not lying!"

"But I gave you my body!" I screamed at the top of my lungs.

"And I appreciate that gift, baby, I—"

"Threw myself at your feet!" I cried. "And now I feel trampled on! Like, you can watch me be in pain and let the shit rock?" I sniffled. "You knew the entire semester that he was with that other girl, that I was the side chick, and you played on my vulnerability to get me." I shook my head.

"No, I didn't—"

"There's nothing you can say to make me feel otherwise. I heard you during your little pissing contest! I heard you!" I swallowed back a sob. "You ain't Broderick to me no more. You ain't shit." I stomped on his foot, pushed the button, and shouldered off the elevator. This was goodbye.

Chapter One

SKYLAR

Four weeks. That's how long it had been. Four weeks ago, I was happy and full of future making bliss. Naïve as hell, too. I was sneakily living in a bubble with my bodyguard turned best friend who became my lover, now, unknowingly, estranged baby daddy. I hadn't uttered a word to him since I left him on the elevator that fateful day. I'd seen him though. He hadn't neglected his obligations to me despite my very vocal wishes that he would. He'd seen me off to classes. I wouldn't get in his car, but he'd trail me every-where that I went. I tried my best to ignore him and eradicate every feeling I have for him. However, remnants of our love lingered in my belly.

"Sky're you sure you want to do this, girl?" Kecia eyed me with nervousness dancing in her orbs.

Her questioning interrupted my thoughts. I was traveling down the intersection of memory lane and defeat. Regret Boulevard was my next turn. She sat nervously to my left, staring me down. Not that I could exactly pay attention to her gaze. I was too busy trying to control my eyes. I was willing myself not to cry— trying to keep my eyes to the wall and ignore the sounds of children in the room. My irises had turned into the bouncing balls that danced atop the television's subtitles. With each beat, they bounced up, trying to avoid the triggering sight of a baby. Finally, I glanced in her direction. I quickly saw her hazel-colored cat eyes. The look in them mirrored mine. My lids began to shutter, and I took a moment to take a deep breath. I hadn't been breathing since I woke up this morning. Not regularly anyway. Just holding the air hostage in my lungs until I could no longer take it. That one, deep breath was followed by several mini breaths, and then more holding. I couldn't focus on breathing at a time like this. My life had gone to hell in a matter of thirty and two days. I didn't know why I was having such a visceral reaction. Hell, I knew what decision I was making. I'd already made the appointment at the clinic. I cringed when they did the ultrasound to check the progress of the fetus. Seeing was believing and I got a huge dose of belief on that table. There was life forming in me – unanticipated life, but life, nonetheless.

I pulled my bottom lip inside my mouth and began to gnaw on the flesh. Opening my eyelids, I averted them to the right of me. I was chewing my lip to smithereens, holding my breath, and staring at the wall.

"You're shaking, Sky," Kecia said in a compassionate voice.

Add shaking to my list of things I was doing. I had to calm myself down or they wouldn't think I was sure about going through with the procedure. *Hell, was I sure?* I knew it was what needed to be done. I had to clip the wings of the future, the disappointment, and the resentment lying within. It was a clear choice. *I can't have this baby.*

At the sound of her tone, I drew in another breath. Her concern was alarming me. I didn't need concern. I didn't need the questioning regard in her eyes. She was trying to make me feel. I didn't have time to feel. I needed to stick to the plan. I needed to be as cold as ice to do something so callous.

"Wilson," I heard the nurse announce in the distance.

A scrawny woman with withered, jet-black hair and her older, female companion gathered their belongs and meandered towards the door. Neither of them looked as spooked as I felt. *Maybe they're here for something else,* I thought.

"Sky..." Kecia called out to me again.

"Kecia, I brought you here because I need a soldier. I knew Jade would try to talk me out of it—plus he knows her car. You're supposed to be the rider today. I already thought about everything. Why do you keep asking me if I'm sure and pointing out my shaking? You think I ain't sure?" I opened my mouth for the first time since being in her presence, but I still wouldn't look at her. I was lying. I was putting on protective armor. If I assured the world that I was confident, they'd back up off me. My gaze returned to the wall. "I'm not a little girl, you know. I'm a grown woman. Grown women make grown decisions." I tried to convince myself more than her.

"Girl, I'm your soldier all day, but I'm also not going to let you make a decision blindly. I won't judge you either way; just think about the fact that if you go through with this, you can't turn back the hands of time," she tried to reason.

"That would be the point of doing it," I murmured, and went back to chewing the skin of my fattened, bottom lip. My attitude wasn't with her. It was with life. I couldn't believe I had gotten myself into this situation. I was a lovesick puppy. Chance's knowledge about Zaïre's betrayal had built a gulf of distance between us. Their pissing match was so embarrassing and hurtful that I could hardly bounce back. And of course, the men were able to continue about their social lives practically unscathed, but me? Every single day there were whispers about me being a "homie hopper" running rampant on campus. No one had the balls to say these things to my face, but the judgmental looks on their faces, the whispers, and seemingly subtle head nods in my direction told it all. I was bleeding internally and had nothing to show for it. I knew once everything came to the forefront, I would get the brunt of the blame, but I was willing to take their darts as long as I had Chance. He was supposed to be my consolation prize. Finding out he was a contributor to my pain sent lightning bolts straight through my chest. They were lodged inside my heart and there was no way for me to ignore it. In my eyes, he was just as fraudulent as Sage. He called often. Texted even more. The nigga even sent cashapps on a regular basis with lines from "Love Jones" in the memo section. I refused to answer, but I stashed the money. Two-thousand dollars sat in my account with his name on it. And although I had my own bread, I took his as a restitution fee. The jig was up. The fat lady had begun to sing. The blinders were off, and I needed distance. I was trying to detox from these niggas. But there was one last thing holding us together. One final tie.

"Girl, don't get mad at me; I'm just trying to help you. Your family might be mad at you at first, but they're going to love you and your child. At least that's what I would expect from the people you rant and rave about. They love you," Kecia said.

The mention of my family sent a tornado of emotions through my heart. Everything I was trying to hold in came to the surface. I stuffed the breath back down my throat and balled my mouth into a tight, shaky frown. I wanted my daddy. He always fixed everything; but even he couldn't fix this. In the careless throws of passion, I had never even given protection a second thought. "Well, if you're trying to help, just be here with me. Damn!" I swore, exasperated by stress. The very existence of this human growing inside of me was gaslighting the shit out of me. The little thing that I was incubating—and without my knowledge prior to the other day—was manipulating me into questioning my own sanity. Was this moment real? Was what I had with Chance real?

"Don't curse at me! You haven't even spoken to him about it. I'm just trying to help you!" Kecia's voice had found the juxtaposition between whispering and yelling, and effectively launched a missile at my heart. "What if he wants the baby? You're not even thinking."

"It's my body. I get to choose," flew out of my mouth. But was I actually choosing? Or was I reacting? Hell, I was terminating the pregnancy for me and for him. We were too young and irresponsible to have a kid.

We didn't even think to put on a condom; how could we remember to change a diaper? We were in college for Christ's sake. We had futures to get to. A baby would only hinder the plan, right?

And speaking of Christ... I hadn't even considered Him until this very moment. *Shit.* Was I stretching the envelope of forgiveness to its maximum capacity? I'd sought forgiveness for fornicating, but was there any room left in His heart for murder? Was I playing God or exercising free will? God *had* to understand that I had to terminate this pregnancy and get my life back on track, right?

I drew another deep breath, and automatically, my foot began to tap the tile in nervous frustration.

"Ok; I'm with you. Your body, your choice," Kecia muttered.

"Lawson," the nurse lady called out for me.

I sipped down my emotion audibly. I had to pull myself together to get this shit done. To face the music. I sat up and drew in another breath. The deepest of the day. I patted my eyes dry with the backs of my still quivering hands.

"Lawson!" The young lady yelled a little louder. Her voice was annoying as hell. Giving a nail to the chalkboard vibe.

I cleared my throat and stood, following her whiney, pitchy tone. I sauntered to her with my head held high.

It wasn't a confident stance. I was merely trying to keep the levee of tears from breaking again.

"Right this way..." She squinted her eyes and affixed them on me. Something about her look was weird. It was laced in judgment—or at least that's how I perceived it. But how could she judge me when she worked here? Hell, if I'm a bad person for getting the procedure done, isn't she worse for facilitating the process? Or was I looking too deeply into it? I shook my head and shrugged off my displaced emotions as the lady extended her hand to usher me. I looked over my shoulder, and spotted Kecia right behind me. *Good. At least I have someone to hold my hand.* I sighed again. *God, help me.*

"Um... I'm sorry, ma'am, she can't come in here with you. She's free to wait in the waiting room though," the nurse lady said.

Great, I thought to myself.

"It's okay, Sky. I'll be out here when you come out," Kecia tried for an upbeat tone. I nodded my head and followed the woman.

When we reached the clammy room, I was ushered to take a seat on the table thing. My legs swung back and forth for the two minutes I'd waited on the doctor.

"Hello, Skylar," Dr. Greene greeted warmly, as if I hadn't just walked into the slaughterhouse.

"Hi," I nodded, barely making eye contact with her.

I didn't want to etch her face into my memory bank. I needed to get in and get out.

"I know we've already done our preliminary chats, but I wanted to briefly go through this talk again. You're opting to have a medical abortion, which is safe and very effective. You'll have two medicines that you need to take: Mifepristone and Misoprostol. First, you'll take the Mifepristone while you're here. Pregnancy needs a hormone called progesterone to grow normally. Mifepristone blocks your body's own progesterone, stopping the pregnancy from growing." She handed me the pill and water. I gazed down at it while listening to the rest of her speech.

"Tomorrow, you're going to take the second medicine, Misoprostol. This medicine causes cramping and bleeding to empty your uterus. It's kind of like having a heavy, crampy period. It's basically a forced miscarriage. And I want to confirm that you have never miscarried before per your medical history, right?" she asked.

I shook my head. "I've never been any of it before. Not pregnant, not miscarried, nothing..." I said faintly.

Dr. Greene eyed me once again. "I just want to make sure you're okay with this."

I took another breath and nodded my head. I had put on the mask of bravery, though I felt anything but it.

"Okay," Dr. Greene nodded. "If you don't have any

bleeding within a day after taking the second medicine, call us and we'll have you come back in, okay?"

I nodded in acknowledgement again.

"I'm also going to prescribe you some Vicodin in case you have pain." Dr. Greene smiled with both eyebrows erect.

I looked at the pill inside my hands and tossed it to the back of my throat. Quickly. I had to do it while I still had the balls. I chased it down with the water, trying to clear the taste of shame from my palette. I gulped it down fiercely.

Moments later, I was but a fragment of myself. A shell. I went out into the lobby and found Kecia sitting alone in the waiting room. The moment I took my seat beside her, a baby began to cry in the distance. Without even trying, my eyes automatically found the chocolate wonder. On sight, the tears I had been holding all morning came streaming from my eyelids like the showers of April. It was only at that moment that I began to mourn what could have been. My chest flew up and crashed back down anxiously. A groan escaped my lips. I couldn't hold it anymore. The violent cry I released warred with the baby's across the room. We howled together in agony, releasing snot bubbles, and pleas for help.

"Oh God," I whispered, while choking on emotion. Those were the only words I could utter. I slumped over, placing my head in between my knees, and cradling it with my trembling hands.

Kecia rubbed my back in circular motions, trying to be of comfort, but there was none to be found. I didn't deserve comforting. I deserved to feel every ounce of pain coming my way. I swallowed it. The pain of judgment, the loss of love, and the stress of having to decide had all culminated in this moment, resulting in the dissolution of life. I couldn't afford to avoid feeling it. Money wouldn't purchase an escape route. Daddy couldn't pray it away. I was swimming in a dark hole of isolation and consequences. Because even after I went through with the act, I hadn't un-mothered. I'd just become the mama of a deceased child. All that was left for me to do was to go to my apartment for the next few days and let the pills take their course.

Chapter Two

CHANCE

I stood right beneath the spout, allowing the water to drench my hair and skin. I was looking rough, real rough. No one had to tell me. I knew it. Hairs were sprouting wildly on my face, and they were left unkempt. If it weren't for practice, I'd be a musty asshole just sitting on my bed wrapped in yesterday's covers. This silent treatment shit with Skylar had me down bad. I ain't never gave not one damn about a woman not speaking to me. In fact, most of my encounters with females were casual, sexual, and at my sole discretion. I set the tone and the pace for every relationship I've ever been in—if you could call them that. They either marched to the beat of my drum or got the fuck on. That was until this little girl from the suburbs came and

13

bulldozed her way into my life. She literally ran into my chest and stayed there. Her cutting me off the last four weeks have been just about unbearable. I tried every single way I could think of to get her to just hear me out. I called and texted her until my fingers just about bled. I sent her money all the time. Although I knew she didn't need a dime from me, I felt the need to send it. I was paying reparations for her tears and her time. And the funniest part was she never sent me the bread back, though she was vehemently ignoring the god. I didn't care about her having the dough though. I'd eat her silence until she got tired. She had to forgive me one day. I mean, I know I hurt her, but it wasn't my intention to. She would have to hear me out—at least I hoped so.

The fact of the matter is, I needed Skylar. Even if she wasn't willing to be my wife, she was already my best friend. I ain't even think I cared about shit like that until her. I had all these relationships with people—my frat brothers, The Supreme Disciples, my blood brothers— but all of them could leave me at the drop of a dime. I would be hurt but move on. I was raised that way. My own mother taught me that niggas leave. It was just life. But I swear the stress that came with losing Skylar had been eating away at my soul like a parasite. She and my OG were the only two people who kept me sane.

These last weeks had been a blur to put it mildly. Basketball's preseason had already begun. I had been breaking ankles on the court since I was a shorty. Between my height and naturally athletic build, putting up buckets was second nature to me. I never took the sport seriously though until now. It was a healthy distraction for me. A legal way to cope. Usually, I would take out my aggressions on the streets.

I serve as the Captain for my grandfather's organization, the Supreme Disciples, and had been doing so since I turned eighteen. My job was to send down orders from the boss and underboss—my OG and Jason—to the soldiers under us. If anybody acted up, it was my job to make niggas pay. My goal was to become an underboss with my brother upon graduating high school, then my OG hit me with this college shit. He was determined for me to go to Davis University. I didn't see the point at all. Yes, I'd always been smart, but I never cared about school —still don't. As Marshawn Lynch once said, "I'm just here so I won't get fined." I was just doing what my grandfather asked of me. He was trying to make me a square, and I ain't with that shit. Executing niggas for their indiscretions and watching these boys become men was my favorite pastime. However, I'd been M.I.A. because of this college shit. I was due to graduate this May. *Thank god.*

I had to get my life back under control. I was off kilter. Between my grandfather's health declining and Skylar's silent treatment, I was on the brink of a nervous breakdown. I hadn't even been active with the Omegas since my blowup with that nigga, Zaïre. All I had was the game of basketball and my classes. I was drained.

I swiveled my head underneath the waterfall, letting the stream from the stainless-steel shower head cleanse my hair and drip down each muscle in my back. DU's athletic facilities were remarkable, state of the art even. The showers were top of the line. The school was known to put big bucks into their athletic and art departments. And while I had played my previous three years at this institution, I'd never taken full advantage of the amenities that came with being a Tiger. Today would be different. After my shower, I planned to get a massage and some of that healthy ass food they sell. Our first game of the season was in a week, and I was trying to detox from all the greasy food I'd been eating all semester.

Thoughts of Skylar flooded my brain like a tsunami as I scrubbed the stench of today's practice from my pores. Her beautiful smile, small waist, and ample ass danced in my mind like a repeated chorus. I missed her. Deeply. Her disrespectful attitude and eyerolls were mainstays in my mind. I'd give anything for her to just curse me out. Instead, she'd chosen to ice me out.

"Aye, Sinclair!" I heard Coach Ross yell, snatching me out of my miserable thoughts.

My head snapped backwards. I was startled to say the least. Turning the knob on the shower to shut it off, I slowly grabbed my towel and wrapped it around my waist to step out of the stall. I heard him yell my name again, but my feet didn't move any faster to see what he wanted. I moved on Chance time. He'd learn that sooner or later.

"What's up, Coach?" I asked as I walked up to him.

Coach Ross was a brown skinned, bigger man. He had to be in his fifties. There was a thick line in between his eyebrows because he frowned often—even when the nigga was happy, he looked pissed off. He had a little hyperpigmentation on his cheeks, and black, carpeted textured hairs with dashes of white for a beard. Buddy was out of shape. You could look at him and tell he had been a star athlete in his day, but his pot belly had replaced the abs he once donned. Despite his stoutness, he was a damn good coach. He always rocked a burgundy polo tucked way too tightly into his belted black jeans. On his head he kept a burgundy baseball cap. His salt and peppered, course hair would always peak out the back and sides when he didn't have a fresh cut. On his feet, he never wore the latest style of sneakers, just some old New Balances. Looking at him, you'd never be able to tell he was a millionaire.

"There's some girl in my gym looking for you," he said, frustrated. "Do I look like a secretary, son?"

"No, sir." I shook my head but was eager to get dressed and head into the gym. The only woman who could be looking for me was Skylar. I'd manifested her presence into my day.

"Then tell your little girlfriends to meet with you on your time. I don't pass messages to players." Coach Ross palmed my shoulder and walked by me.

Scurrying back to the locker room, I halfway dried off and slipped on my white, Versace t-shirt, matching boxer briefs, and blue jeans. I misted myself with Creed cologne with my right hand while trying to put my shoes on my feet with my left. I tossed all my shit in my duffle bag while simultaneously checking myself out in the mirror. I wish I'd gotten my hair cut, but sadness at the loss of our relationship had consumed me. I hadn't made the time to get my brother to cut it. Regardless, I looked pretty good and smelled even better.

Power walking, I found my way into the gym. With each step I took as I neared my desired location, my chest blossomed with adoration for my girl. I wish I had gotten her some flowers or something. A romantic gesture of some sort. That's what I knew she liked. That corny shit. I knew all I had to do was see her and we'd work it out. Skylar's my wife—my world. If she'd just put eyes on me, I knew she couldn't resist our chemistry. It was visceral and powerful enough to mold us together. We just had to see one another. That's why she was avoiding me—ignoring me. She knew, like I knew, we belonged together.

Once I bent the corner, everything stopped. There were only about thirty people in the gym, but only one was there specifically to see me. My steps slowed and anger set in the pit of my stomach. *How the hell did this girl even know where I was?*, I wondered. Nicole stood in a black, North Face hoodie, blue denim booty shorts, and rain boots. They were Prada, but rain boots, nonetheless. Her fair skin was puffy and red in the face. I didn't care why she was here; I just knew I didn't want to see her. *And I done sprayed my good cologne for nothing.*

"What're you doing here, Nicole?" I asked. There were no niceties in my tone. I was cut and dry. I had not spoken to her since the kickback, and we weren't about to start back kicking it now.

"Still rude I see," Nicole rolled her eyes.

"I ain't ask you what you see. I asked you what you want," I ice grilled her.

Nicole scoffed. "You're impossible," her eyes coated with tears. "I wanted to know if I could speak to you in private."

I shook my head, "Hell nah. My girl ain't going for that. Just say what you got to say."

Nicole's head rolled back as if she had been punched in her face. I wasn't sure why. Since the incident with Zaïre, everyone on this campus knew what it what between Skylar and me. The whispers hadn't stopped at all. No one knew where she and I stood currently, but that wasn't their business.

"Your girl?" Her face grew fire hydrant red. "So, it's true?"

"Is that what you came up here for?" I asked, nonchalantly.

"I came to talk to you!" she yelled. "But you're sitting here confirming to me that this chick, who you claimed was just your *best friend,* is your quote-unquote girl? How long has this been the case? Because I was just sitting on it two months ago, Chance!"

My eyes glanced around the gymnasium. This girl was embarrassing as hell. I ain't need nobody to know my business like that. "Calm yo' ass down," I warned through clenched teeth. "I ain't got to answer shit. I ain't with you—I never was, never will be. That's all you need to know. Now, you got about seven seconds to tell me what the hell you want, and I'm being generous because I feel bad for you. It's clear you're confused. For one, you think you can question me about mine; for two, you're dressed for three seasons in one outfit. Now, what is it? You about to make me tight."

"Chance," her eyes pleaded with me.

"Just say it!" My thunderous voice shook the building. I was so tired of this girl I didn't know what to do. I didn't want to disrespect her, but she refused to take 'no' for an answer.

"Fine!" Her right hand reached inside the left bra cup and pulled out a white device. "I'm pregnant, you selfish, arrogant, egotistical asshole!" She slammed the pregnancy test into my chest. This hoe whipped the test out like she was Amina Butterfly, and my name was Peter Gunz from Love and Hip Hop.

I heard gasps surrounding the both of us. My right hand instinctively dropped my duffle bag and grabbed the test. I just kept looking between her and it. Then her again then it. The pregnancy test had a clear "plus" sign staring back at me. *What is she trying to say?*

"The hell you telling me for? I strapped up every single time, b." I bit my lip. I had never even remotely slipped up with this girl. How was this possible?

"I'm telling you because you're the only man I've been with in the last year. I'm telling you so you can take care of your responsibilities when the time comes! I'm telling you because you're about to be a daddy!" Nicole was bawling and yelling. By now, everyone in the building knew about our drama.

Embarrassed, I grabbed my duffle bag and put it over my shoulder. "I won't know shit 'til I get a DNA test."

I saw it. The moment her heart sank. In the very next second, I saw an evil gleam in her eyes. "I will get the test done in utero." She kissed her teeth. "I knew you weren't all the way fond with me since that girl got on this campus, but I will never forgive you for treating me this way. You're going to pay! I wonder what Skylar's going to think when she finds out her *man* has a baby on the way."

"Keep my wife's name out yo'…"

"Sinclair!" I heard Coach Ross holler my name right before I was about to go Will Smith on her ass.

"Yes, sir, Coach."

"I need to see you in my office," he paused. "Now!"

He was rescuing me from going to prison for ringing this girl's neck. Skylar's name coming from her mouth sounded like hot shit on a summer's day. I couldn't stomach the sound. She was threatening to tell her about this pregnancy that I didn't know for sure was real, or mine for that matter. If it was, my life was over. I could kiss my wife goodbye. There was no way she was going for that. Just a second ago, I was missing my girl; now, I'm afraid I'll never get her back. "Get you some help, sweetheart," I shrugged my shoulders, trying to be cool, but deep inside, I was anything but it.

"Get your child support ready, baby daddy," she mocked me as I walked out of the gym.

As soon as I got to Coach's office, he shut the door behind us.

"Son, tell me you didn't get that girl pregnant," he rubbed his eyes.

I shrugged. "All I know is I have this test," I held it in my hand. "I don't know for sure if *she* is the one who actually took this, if the kid is mine, or nothing!" I rattled off at the chest.

"Did you have unprotected sex with this young lady?" he asked.

"I always strapped up with her, Coach. No slip ups," I shook my head. "I don't know what I'm gon' do. My girl is going to kill me!" For the first time since hearing the news, tears stung my eyes.

"Wait, you have a girlfriend who is not that young lady? Aww hell! You haven't even made it to the Pro's yet and you're already on your way to becoming Tristen Thomson II," Coach snatched his hat off and scratched his head. "Dammit, this won't be good!"

"The Pro's?" I scoffed.

"Yeah, the Pro's. I've been telling you for three years you have the skill to be a professional athlete, but you won't take yourself seriously enough to get there. I would hate to see you get into that arena and watch you become another statistic, creating broken homes in the Black community," he shook his head. "I have someone I want to take you up under his wing. His name is Edward Stenton..."

"The point guard for the Bulls?" I questioned.

"Yeah, him. He's an alumnus. I feel like he can help mentor you. You're a good athlete but if you take your-self more seriously and get the right coaching and mentorship, you can become the 2021 version of Magic Johnson, pre-HIV."

I shook my head at his inappropriate comment.

"Well, at the rate you're going—"

"Chill, Coach," I interrupted him before he pissed me off. "I'll meet with the bull."

AFTER TALKING WITH MY COACH, I DROVE UP TO The Angelous. I pulled right up on the curb, parked on the sidewalk, and watched people going in and out like a weirdo. Every time a person walked past my car, they whispered about my strangeness. I didn't care though. I had to make sure Nicole didn't walk her humpty dumpty ass in there and try to talk to my lady. I couldn't have that. I had to be the one to talk to her first. The problem was, *how could I do that? What would I say? How would she react? Would she even let me inside her apartment? How would I even get a chance to tell her what was going on when she wasn't speaking to me?* Question on top of question rattled my mind. An unidentifiable emotion had washed over me. For once in my life, I didn't know what to do. I needed reinforcement. I needed someone to tell me how to deal out this news in such a way where she would not leave me.

Biting the skin off my bottom lip, I decided to call

my brothers—Jason and LJ. If it were any other woman, I would have called Lil Steve, seeing as though that nigga is on the track to get married, has a kid, and a bunch of them on the way. He'd be the perfect man to talk to about getting a woman to take you back. I remember when he had me following his woman around about a year ago when they'd broken up. Lil Steve had messed up royally, but somehow, he was able to get his woman back and create an even tighter family unit with her. That's what I wanted with Sky. Some Michael and Jay Kyle, My Wife and Kids, type shit. But calling Lil Steve was out seeing as though the woman in pursuit was his baby sister. I already knew that he would one day find out about us, and it would be curtains for me. When the time came, I would have to face it like a man; but until then, all I had to worry about was her.

Touching the green icon on my phone, I FaceTimed Jason and LJ on three-way. The first to answer was Jason. I could tell he was driving because he had the phone in the cupholder. All I could see was his shoulders, head, and long, right arm extended on the wheel. His hair was faded, and the lining was as straight as an arrow—just crispy. I could see the gray and black, plaid blazer he rocked with a white shirt. Jason is my only blood sibling, but we couldn't be more different. The nigga always dressed like he was going to church or court. My ass dressed like I belong on the court.

"What up, nigga?" he asked, while turning down his blasting music.

"Nigga, why you listening to 'Good Morning Gorgeous'? You got something you need to share with the group? Ole sensitive ass," I poked fun at him.

"Hell, naw," Jason scoffed. "I can't even spell vulnerable." We fell out laughing. "Nah, Khadijah had my car earlier. That's her music."

My eyes bugged out of my head. Jason wasn't that type. His cars were very distinguishable. They were all custom painted in matte black. I had never seen him allow another human to push his car, let alone a woman —and he kept plenty of them around. However, he was sitting here telling me that one of his women, who happens to be Lil Steve's old lady's best friend, had been riding around the city in his shit?

"Word?" I asked.

Before Jason could answer, LJ chimed into the call. "What y'all ass want? I'm not in the mood." I chuckled at the scowl on his face. Meanwhile, Jason ignored him. LJ was probably just hungry. He was always moody as hell when he got hungry. We were cousins, but I looked at him as my second brother. His face was directly in the camera. Far too close. All I saw was nostrils and lips. "Aye, let me get a mini tip with extra sauce. I need my meat swimming in sauce. I don't want to see no brown, only red. You got me?"

"Yes, sir. Would you like anything else?" I could hear the clerk say in a sultry tone.

"Let me get two Pepsi's and ten wings, too, sweetheart. That's it," he ordered.

"Who finna eat all that damn food, b?" I inquired.

"Yo', you in my business. Don't do that," LJ said and pulled his hoodie down further to cover his eyes.

"Yo'! I ain't got all day," Jason groaned. "I got moves to make. What you call us for, bruh?"

I looked outside the window, watching fellow students maneuver their way around my car, which was parked in their way. Sighing heavily, I tried to think of the words to say.

"If you don't just spit it the hell out!" LJ's grumpy self complained.

"Fine. Y'all remember that chick, Nicole?" I questioned.

"The chick you was bangin' from the kickback? What about her?" LJ asked.

"Yeah..." I paused. "She came to my basketball practice and made a big ass scene." I held up the pregnancy test she slammed into my chest. "Shorty claims I got her pregnant."

"The fuck?" Jason's car swerved a little to the right. The announcement got him so surprised he almost lost control of the car.

"Nigga, what?" LJ exclaimed. "When was this?"

"Jason, be careful, nigga!" I chastised him.

"*You* be careful, withcha dumb ass!" Jason yelled and pulled over. I could see the steam rising from his ears.

"Again, when was this?" LJ pinched his nose in frustration.

"About three hours ago," I retorted, while rolling the test between my fingers. I couldn't believe it.

"And yo' nasty ass just sitting there, twirling a pissy pregnancy test like it's nothing. Just pissy, nasty, and dumb simultaneously, huh? Don't tell nobody else you're my brother, nigga. You're straight up embarrassing," Jason exclaimed. "You ain't strap up with this hoe?"

"Hell yeah!" I exclaimed. "I ain't stupid. I kept a box of condoms in her damn room to ensure that I stayed strapped up!"

Both Jason and LJ looked at me and busted out laughing. They were in hysterics. My brows furrowed in confusion.

"What y'all laughing at?" I pondered.

"You!" Jason exclaimed.

"Time out, time out!" LJ hooted while grabbing his food. "Let me get this straight, g. You know you have a crazy girl who likes you a lot, wants to be your woman, and clearly has low self-esteem because she lets you talk to her crazy and she comes back for more. She's proven herself to be mentally unstable, yet you entrust her solely with the responsibility of not conceiving your offspring? You leave your protection in her hands, and you're surprised that she's with child. Is that what you're telling us, bro?"

I combed my fingers through my budding beard. I hadn't thought about it like that. I had given this girl the task to cover us—the duty to make sure I didn't impregnate her—but it was my job to protect my own future. It was my job to be a man. I was culpable.

"Maaaan…" I dragged out the word while wiping my hands down my face.

Jason shook his head. "Did you at least see her take the test? That could be her friend's test or anything. And furthermore, how does she know it's yours?"

I shook my head. "Nah, she just brought me the positive test. And I won't know if the kid is mine until we get a DNA test."

Jason scoffed. "I got another question, dumbass."

"I think I got the same question, bro," LJ chimed in.

"What?" I groaned. This entire situation was already frustrating. Their insults were further pissing me off.

"Does Baby Girl know?" Jason asked, referring to Skylar.

My head dropped immediately. I was ashamed. I was angry. I was confused.

"Nah, that's why I called y'all. I know she's going to

be pissed when she finds out about this. Ole girl threated to tell her..."

"Oh, heeeeeell no," LJ interrupted. "She needs to hear that from your mouth. You can't let that ditzy broad go anywhere near her."

"Facts," I agreed. "That's why I'm parked outside our apartment complex now, making sure Nicole doesn't get to her before I can; but I can't seem to get out this car and talk to her. She's already angry with me. I know when I tell her about an impending baby, she's gon' be tight as hell."

"Tight?" Jason shook his head. "I tried to put every ounce of game I had inside you; and here you go, messing it up.

"Skylar ain't just gon' be mad that you're having a kid on her, it's going to rip her heart out her chest. That's a pain you can't apologize away. At the end of the day, every time she sees that baby, she's going to remember your stupidity, stupid," Jason stressed.

"Aye! I ain't gon' be too many more stupids," I warned.

"Then stop being stupid as hell, stupid," Jason barked. "Who you think you talkin' to? I ain't your baby mama! That's why I ain't want you to get with Baby Girl anyway. I knew you would fuck it up. Not only is Lil Steve gon' kill you for dating her in the first place, but they're going to tag team you when she finds out about this betrayal."

My upper lip curled.

"J, chill man," LJ intervened while biting a piece of the rib tip. "Chance knows he was stupid; you ain't got to rub it in, bro."

I shook my head.

"Now, were you cheating on Sky?" LJ asked.

My chest puffed out. I was offended by the question. LJ's eyes read sincere, but he had me fucked up. "I would never cheat on my lady. Ever. We don't have those problems. *If* this girl is pregnant, it happened before we got together."

Jason sighed.

"Well, that's a selling point. Perhaps you can use it while you're begging forgiveness," LJ pointed his saucy finger into the camera. "You were trapped, and it was before her."

I nodded, taking in his words.

"Well, all the best to you. If she doesn't kill you, call us to tell us how it went," LJ uttered.

"You need to make that girl take a test in front of you," Jason warned.

"I got you," I nodded and hung up. I felt worse now than I had before I called.

Taking the car out of park and into drive, I found a

legitimate parking space and trekked up the stairs. I was so nervous I didn't want to take the elevator. I couldn't. I couldn't stand still. Instead, I ran up the stairs, skipping every other one until I got to her floor. Once I landed at her door, I took an exhausted, deep breath. I needed a second to get my thoughts together. *How am I going to start?* I decided to just go. I banged on the door with my right fist.

"Sky, baby," I called after her, and was met with silence. "Bae, I know you don't want to talk to me, but I need you. Can you just give me five minutes?" I could see in the cracks of the door that the lights were on. She was home—I could feel her presence on the opposite side of the door—she just didn't want to answer. I put my forehead up to the door, distraught. "Bae, I'm sorry." I could hear whimpering on the other side of the door. The sound of her cries made my heart crack into pieces. She was a pit bull in a dress; Skylar wasn't a crier like that, so to hear her cry played with my mental. "Don't cry, baby. We can work this out. Just you and me. Just open the door."

"I thought I asked you to leave me alone, Chance," Sky wept. The sound of her voice sent lightning bolts through my belly that shot straight to my heart. The quivers in her voice made me feel like a bigger douche bag. This wouldn't be the last tear she cried. "I just need time. Please, respect me. I don't want to talk."

"I know, baby, but there's something I need to share

with you. I need my best friend. Can you do that for me? Can you let me talk to my best friend for two minutes? I ain't trying to keep nothing else from you. I need to talk to you, love." I begged. Me. It's never happened before. Only a real woman can bring a man to his knees. I was being vulnerable, and the ball was in her court. I couldn't make her talk to me. I could only beg.

Before I could utter another word, I saw the lights go out, and heard footsteps walking in the distance. There was my answer. She wasn't willing to hear me out; but I also wasn't willing to let this go that easily. *She gon' talk to me!* I pouted inwardly while sliding down to cop a seat on the floor. I pulled out my phone and began to watch YouTube videos. I knew she had a class this evening; so, I was willing to sit in this spot, right outside her door, because we were fixing things *tonight.* Yeah, my OG had been right. I'm a "sucka", as he would call it, a simp even, and I'd be that for Skylar.

Chapter Three

SKYLAR

The medically induced miscarriage was a two-day process. After getting home from the clinic, I was fine. Kecia agreed to stay the night in my apartment, so I didn't have to be alone. I truly thanked God for her. I knew Jade would probably be upset that I hadn't brought her along this journey, but honestly and truthfully, her sister had created a wedge in our relationship. She was still my friend and I still loved her, but I didn't want to put her in any tough situations. Sage, her twin, was an idiot, and I didn't need her taking her frustrations with me out on her sister. She was that type. Jade and I still texted, and I still considered her as one of my friends, but if there had to be a side to stand on, why would I expect her to stand with me against her perfidious sister? It still blew my mind that I have not heard a peep from Sage, though I have seen her around campus being arm-in-arm with Taylor. Taylor, the girl my ex-boyfriend cheated on me with. Sage knew of his betrayal the entire time, even befriended the girl, yet she pretended to be a friend of mine. She even went as far as questioning my relationship with Chance all while knowing I was being played. The girl was a snake and a crook. It was also clear that she was insanely jealous of me. At every turn, she never missed an opportunity to talk about how snobbish and stuck up she believed I was because I grew up with money and she didn't. Sage was the kind of frenemy who would have a wet dream because she saw you stumble; meanwhile, Jade was the epitome of a pillar of support. How they both came from the same egg was beyond me.

Regardless, I made a mental note to contact Jade once the pain subsided. When we came back from the clinic, I was fine...physically, that is. I was still emotional about the decision I had made, but what was done was done. Or at least, it was being done. Kecia kept asking me how I was doing, which was irritating, but appreciated. We'd decided to watch my favorite movie and order a pizza. Now why would I do that to myself?

"You think you're with the woman you're 'sposed to be with?" Darius asked.

"Haha," Von laughed. "That question implies some

belief in destiny, like some cosmic love connection and I'm not convinced anymore."

"I'm just asking a question," Darius replied.

"So, you asking me if I married my soulmate?"

"Yeah."

Von scoffed, "Depends on which day you ask."

"Dig that."

"Doesn't really matter anymore, man. You're with who you're with. You just gotta try to make it work."

"Real deep, Von, real deep."

"Well, you know people with profound insights on life know not to get married. And those who do —well, they know that marriage is what you make it." Von paused. "This is about that girl Nina, isn't it?"

"What you doing, man? Can I get my shot?"

"No no no no no no... This is about that girl Nina, right?" Von reiterated as Darius attempted to shoot his shot on the pool table.

Darius cleared his throat.

"She jacked you up, didn't she?" Von asked with a knowing smile.

"She jacked me up, man," Darius admitted.

I CHUCKLED WHILE SUBTLY WIPING THE TEAR that crept out of the corner of my right eye. I was supposed to be getting full on Home Run Inn and chuckling at the fact that Darius and Nina couldn't get their stuff together and swooning when they finally had. Instead, this motion picture film was triggering the heck out of me. So many of these moments felt familiar. My life had imitated the art. It was deeper than our first date —though I, too, had sex with my man on the first date— it was more so about their connection, the heat, and the stumbling blocks that stood in their way.

I cracked a smile when Darius lied and said his famous line, "We just kickin' it."

"One truism in life my friend: when that jones come down, it be a mofo," I quoted and censored Von's witty advice. "You ain't wrong, Von," I testified to the television as if Isaiah Washington could hear me. "Ain't wrong at all."

I could feel the burning sensation of someone staring at me. I turned my head slowly and caught eyes with Kecia. She was looking puzzled, so I grabbed the remote control and hit the pause button. I don't miss moments of Love Jones. Not a bit or a piece of it could be discarded, no matter how many times I'd seen the film.

"Why're you looking at me like that?" I asked as I nervously tugged on my pink pajama sleeve.

"You know, we haven't known each other long, but I'm starting to look at you like you're slow," she said blankly.

"Say what now?" I sat up defensively.

"Friend, if you miss that nigga that much, just call him. Yes, he was wrong for not telling you about your scallywag of a friend, but deep down inside, you already knew she wasn't your real friend. What, you were looking for physical proof of it?"

That layer of truth caught me in the throat. Initially, I sat there dumbfounded until I could think of a comeback. "First of all, who said I missed him?"

Kecia looked at me and her face folded, as if she thought I was dumb. "Girl, I'm trying hard to blame that question on your hormonal imbalance due to your procedure because there ain't no way you don't know that I can see you crying because you miss the nigga."

I shrugged. "Ok; fine, I miss him; but it's deeper than Sage. He knew about Zaïre cheating; he also knew that Sage was a witness to his betrayal. I'm embarrassed. Everybody was in on the joke but me. How was Chance my supposed best friend but he kept that information from me? Honestly, I was hurting every day because I knew I was falling for Brod—Chance, but I kept those boundaries there because I was being loyal to Zaïre's cheating ass. And for Chance to know and not say anything, for him to see me be hurt by this nigga and not say anything, was a big deal for me. We were better than that."

Kecia shrugged. "And I agree with that. I'm not

invalidating your feelings, but y'all can talk that stuff out. *He* didn't cheat on you."

"But he knew," I interrupted her. "I don't deal with too much disloyalty. When I see it in the slightest, I cut niggas off," I stated. "And Chance *knows* more than anyone the code of honor and loyalty. He chose to not be those things with me."

"Well, I think y'all can fix it. I'll understand if you don't tell him about the abortion but share your feelings with him. He clearly wants to work on things. He keeps blowing your phone up all day and sending you cashapps. Man, I wish I had that with Jamel. That nigga treated my heart like a literal toy. Do you know how long it took me to get him out of my system?"

"How long?" I asked, intrigued.

Kecia bit her lower lip. "About a year and a half. I kept letting him come back, even though there were no signs that he was willing to change."

I reached over and rubbed her hand. She was clearly affected by this story. "What happened with you guys?"

She shrugged. "Girl, Jamel was a wolf in sheep's clothing. He started off a great guy. I met him at Trinity High School in tenth grade. We were both students. He was a popular dude because he was a hustler. I wasn't popular at all. I was always quiet. I grew up in the foster care system, so I knew how to be by myself pretty well. Because I performed so well academically, I became a tutor to make some money on the side. This nigga was as dumb as a box of rocks when it came to science, so I tutored him. Slowly but surely, we started catching feelings for one another. I was book smart, but his tenure in the streets had him running lightyears ahead of me in the commonsense department.

"Jamel and I were good until we weren't. I don't know what the catalyst was, but suddenly, I couldn't do anything right. He would yell at me and call me names when we got into it. He even started putting his hands on me," Kecia teared up.

"Ugh," I reached over to her and rubbed her back. "I'm sorry, friend. I have a sister who was in an abusive relationship, too."

"Yeah well, at least your sister had enough sense to leave. I stayed for a while, and I don't even know why. Well, I take that back. I thought I could love the demons out of him."

"Wow," I whispered.

"Things got worse when his older brother was killed. Before, he would always apologize after a fight or give me gifts. After his brother, he just became paranoid and evil," she said.

"Evil like what?"

"Like, we got into an argument the night his brother passed. We moved in together during my senior year. His family came over to our place when his brother was killed. I was hosting everyone, trying to make sure they were comfortable—especially his mother. Jamel was drunk and I was trying to make him lie down. Big mistake. He started accusing me of wanting to get rid of him, cheating on him, and all type of foolishness."

"Girl, what?" I asked.

"Yeah," she shook her head. "He started fighting me like I was a man off the street in front of his family, who did nothing but watch. That's when I knew it would never change. If he would knock me out in front of his own mother, he was comfortable, comfortable."

"That's wild."

"It is. I left him the next day after feeding him a sleeping pill," she shrugged. "I ran away and never returned. Now, see, that's some real relationship drama. What you're going through is amenable. Chance seriously loves you—he ain't putting hands on you, disrespecting you, or cheating on you. He made a bad choice. We all do that. Stop letting your ego ruin your happiness and talk to that man."

I paused, taking in each word that poured from her wise fountain. I shifted around in my seat. The cramps had started to come, and I could feel the process taking its course. "Okay," I reluctantly consented. Everything Kecia said I took to heart. It was true. I was allowing my ego to keep this going. "I'll at least hear him out; but it'll have to be next week because these cramps are getting the best of me," I groaned.

"Oh no!" Kecia exclaimed. She got up and frantically started moving back and forth, looking for something to do. "Girl, what am I supposed to get you? How we rockin'? Do I need to call the amalance?"

I hissed through the pain. "Nigga, you too old, smart, and accomplished to be mispronouncing ambulance. Now, sit your ass down and hold my hand. I'm going to try and get some sleep."

"Do you need to change your pad?" she asked.

I shook my head. The sound of my vibrating phone startled the both of us. Looking down at my phone, I saw the name "Broderick" dancing across the screen with a heart emoji. I gasped and looked up at Kecia. "It's him!"

"Aww shit! He just *knows* something is going down! He's going to kill you! Double homicide!" Kecia panicked.

"Girl, shut up!" I tried my best not to laugh as I sent his call to voicemail. Suddenly, I heard a knock at my door. Kecia and I froze in place. Chance had been doing a good job of giving me my space—even though he called and texted—but not now. He was demanding to talk to me. I knew it was him. I could feel him through the door.

"Sky, baby," He called out.

I eyed Kecia with tears in my eyes. No way could I let him in this door while I was actively ridding myself of his baby. *God, why are you doing this to me?*

"Bae, I know you don't want to talk to me, but I need you. Can you just give me five minutes?"

I heard the desperation in his voice. The way I wanted to run into his arms and make him rub my back and my feet right now. I needed this nigga; but there was no way I could let him in.

"Talk to him," Kecia whispered.

"I can't!" I pointed down to my abdomen. "Go turn the light out."

"That's dumb! He'll be able to see you turning the lights off."

"Look, can you just do what I asked?" Tears welled up in my eyes. I needed him to think I was still shutting him out and go away.

I heard knocks at the door again, which caused me to close my eyes tightly in angst. I could hear Kecia scurry to the lights. As soon as she hit them, I heard Chance sigh.

"Bae, I'm sorry."

Him calling out to me tore my heart out. I was getting rid of the last pieces of us while he was on the other side battling to piece us together. My silent tears began to be laced with sounds. Soft whimpers involuntarily bled from my mouth. Kecia ran over and hugged me as I began to sob. I had never cried as much as I had in the last few weeks.

"Don't cry, baby," I heard him say. "We can work this out. Just you and me. Just open the door."

Seeing he wasn't going to leave until he heard my voice, I spoke up. "I thought I asked you to leave me alone, Chance." My pleas were pregnant with tears. My lips quivered as I plead my case through closed eyes. "I just need time. Please, respect me. I don't want to talk."

"I know, baby, but there's something I need to share with you. I need my best friend. Can you do that for me? Can you let me talk to my best friend for two minutes? I ain't trying to keep nothing else from you. I need to talk to you, love," he begged. Chance was begging. That wasn't him. He'd never begged for anything, yet he was begging me. This time, I couldn't oblige his request. After growing weary from his supplication and my own physical pain, I slowly lifted myself from the couch to go into the bedroom. I'd almost forgotten about Kecia, which was to be expected. When I was with Chance, no one else mattered. No one else was there. We had the type of love that edged out extras. I could feel nothing but our magnetic energies drawing us toward one another. Unfortunately for us, we couldn't pull together this time. We were pulling a part.

"Sky!" I felt Kecia shaking my body, waking me up out of my slumber.

A groan escaped my mouth. I had been cramping all night. I barely got any sleep. It felt like the most intense menstrual cycle I had ever experienced. The physical pain coupled with my emotional turmoil had kept me up all night. By the time I had fallen asleep, I'd had a nightmare. Kecia had no idea she was waking me up from a hell storm. In the dream, three babies were chasing me down the highway. I was completely naked, running down the street. Somehow, I tripped and fell, and the babies started attacking me. The feeling of Kecia's hand shook me out of my slumber and caused my eyes to pop open.

"I got class. I was about to leave, but your nigga is at the door," she said.

My eyes bugged out of my head. "Huh?"

"Girl, that nigga must've slept in your hallway. He's lying across the threshold with his phone in his hand. He is knocked out. You got to go talk to him now," she said. "And clean yourself up." She pointed at the blood in my bed. That's when I noticed. The process had to have happened.

Meanwhile, this psychopath hadn't left my place at all last night. I rushed to the toilet to handle my business, and then to the sink to address my hygiene. Quickly, I went into the living room where Kecia was sitting, waiting on me to move this ridiculously tall man from my threshold so she could leave.

I swung the heavy door open to find him asleep on his back, with a scowl on his countenance. His phone was in his right hand, which was crossed over his peanut head. My baby looked rough. Like he had been going through it. *Good.* It felt good to know he was suffering without me. He'd grown a stubble-filled beard and his eyebrows were a little wild. I was going to take him out of his misery today. Today would be the day when we spoke and got our union on one accord. Kecia was right. I was letting my ego and embarrassment get in the way of our happiness together. Looking down at him, I saw forever in his chocolate skin.

Kecia cleared her throat, reminding me of her presence. I looked up at her and back down at him, about to wake him up. I instantly got pissed off when I saw his morning wood on display for my entire floor to see. Kecia ain't need to see what my man was working with. I picked up my right foot and kicked him in the side with the swiftness.

"Get your ass up!" I yelled.

Chance shot up and went for the waist of his jeans until he realized it was me. "Is you serious right now? You almost got your ass killed!" He looked at me through bewildered eyes.

"Boy, ain't nobody thinking about you!" I shot and

47

stood directly in front of him to block Kecia's view of him. I already had a girl mess with my last man, I wasn't letting it happen again.

Kecia scoffed. "Girl, I'm out. Talk to this nigga because both of y'all are insane. Bye Chance," she said and started down the hall. His rude ass didn't even respond.

"You wanted to talk?" I turned to face him.

He didn't verbally say a word; instead, he shouldered past me and headed into my place. I could already tell he was going to be on some bull.

"Chance, I..." I started, but he kept walking until he reached the bathroom and closed the door. *Rude as always.* I began to pace the floors until he came out and grabbed me by my hands. I could smell the mint from his tongue from where I stood. "Did you use my toothbrush."

"Yeah," he shrugged. "Is that a problem?"

My face folded immediately. I looked at him like he was stupid. "Yeah, nigga. That's nasty! I don't want to be sharing mouth germs with you. You could have gingivitis."

His head drew back in offense. "If I got gingivitis, then why would you let me put my tongue in every hole, crevasse, and fold of your body?"

Stunned at his jab, my lips automatically formed an

"o" and my nipples pebbled at the thought of the places his tongue had explored.

"But none of that matters right now," he said as he sat down and grabbed me to sit with him. Chance sat me down on his lap, one of my favorite places to be. Feeling slightly nervous that he would feel my pad, maneuvered onto my hip and laid my face on his chest, letting him cradle me. I needed to be here after just going through the painful experience of terminating a life. I needed his arms around me; so, when he grabbed me by the hands and looked at me in the eyes, I acquiesced swiftly. "I need to talk to you, love."

"I know," I said softly. I had been so hard for weeks; but now that I was finally in his presence, inhaling his masculine musk, feeling his velvety skin, and peering into his soul's windows, my powerful veneer had been stripped from me. I was reduced to a needy girl who loved her man in mere moments. I was willing to work it out with him now that I'd seen him. It was what I'd been avoiding all along. I knew that one touch from Chance would have me reneging on every tough girl affirmation I'd given myself. I was drunk in love with this nigga. "I need to talk to you, too. You hurt me, Broderick."

Chance closed his eyes and let his head fall back onto the wall. I'm guessing it was because I'd let his real name slip. He loved when I called him by his government. It was our thing. I hadn't even thought about it. I'd said it because I knew in this moment I was getting my Broderick back. He'd come to restore order—or so I thought until he closed his eyes. He'd shut his eyes, his beautifully brown eyes, revoking my access to his innermost parts. "I know, and I'm sorry. I don't want to keep hurting you..."

"Then don't," I interrupted him and circled my arms around his neck. "Just promise me you won't hurt me again and we can move forward." I knew that was a lot to ask for. We were humans. Humans hurt one another without even trying; but I wouldn't be able to stomach hurt from Chance. He was my lifeline. I needed protection from him. That's how we'd started off. He was my protector. I needed him to shield me from anything that would harm me—even if that meant shielding me from himself. I needed him to be superhuman for me. To live up on a pedestal. Men hurt women every day, but I needed my superhuman to go harder for me. To be the exception to the rule.

"Babe—," he said through shut eyes. It came out more like a groan, like he was in pain.

"What's the deal?" I asked, confused. "Just promise me. Just open your eyes and promise me."

Chance took a beat, then opened his eyes. They were bloodshot red and glossy. I had only seen him tear up about his grandfather's diagnosis. Not even conversations about the abuse he experienced at the hands of his mother had caused him to break down. I went into panic mode.

"Is your OG okay?" I asked as my eyes searched his body for some type of clue.

He nodded.

"Then why are you about to cry? Are you okay?"

He shut his eyes again and one, lone tear seeped out.

"It's you," he cleared his throat and said.

"Me? What about me?" I begged. "Can you just open your eyes and tell me."

Chance took a deep, cleansing breath and wiped his eye in the most toxic way I had ever seen. It was as if he were beating the tear for falling out. "Uh... I love you. And I'm just upset that I'm about to lose the best thing that's ever happened to me."

I began to blink excessively. I removed my arms from his shoulders and crossed them over my body. Fortifying myself. Building the wall back up. Whatever he was getting ready to tell me was about to break us—to break me. "What the hell did you do?" I accused.

Chance manned up and finally looked me in the eye. "Nicole came to the gym yesterday and said she was pregnant and that the kid is mine."

"Excuse me?" I questioned my sanity and my hearing at the same time. There was no way on God's green earth that this was happening right now.

"She's pregnant, Nicole is. She claims it's mine but—"

"It's yours," I whispered and shot off his lap until my hunches came crashing to the floor. I knew the kid was his because of my dream. Three kids were chasing me down, killing me in my dream. One of them was mine. "Y'all must be having twins," I thought aloud. I tried to take a deep breath, but my chest was locked.

"Baby..." Chance got up from the sofa and walked toward me.

The second he touched me, a scream so high-pitched and piercing erupted from my body. My entire frame shook as I began to sob, realizing what had just been spoken. "You fucked her while you were making love to me?" I screamed and questioned him. Blows from my fists came crashing on his back while I questioned him. "You scum bag! You was screwing her raw!"

"Hell no!" Chance screamed and bear hugged me, trying to stop my attempts to hit him. My entire body was bucking wildly in his hold. "I have not slept with that girl since I got with you, and I always strapped up. That's my word."

Upon hearing that information, I began to weep in his arms.

"I'm sorry this is hurtful, but I would never cheat on you. It happened literally right before you," he said as the tears poured from my eyes. "I know you hate me now, but I swear I didn't cheat on you. In a few months, we can get a DNA test, baby."

He thought I was crying because of his new baby. No. It wasn't just that. I was crying because of what could have been. I compromised my soul for a future that should've been spent with him. Now she was gaining everything I thought I would have with the guy I wanted it all with. She was unapologetically baring his seed while I hastily extinguished mine.

CHANCE

Skylar pulled away from me and just stared into my eyes. Agony danced in her orbs like a raisin in the sun. She was hurt. I was hurt.

"I wouldn't be selfish enough to ask you to stick with me through this," I shook my head.

Skylar scoffed.

"But I had to tell you because I didn't want you to get this information from anybody else. Especially her," I paused and looked at her blank eyes. "I'd planned to marry you one day. I wanted us to be like the new version of my OG and Grandma. I wanted you to be the mother of my children."

I watched her visibly shutter at the last mention.

"I wanted the white picket fence and to retire from the streets with you. I wanted to teach our future sons how to play basketball and how to talk to women. I wanted to do all that corny shit you like doing, like dressing alike for events and holidays," I stroked her cheek. "I wanted all those things with you." I sighed. "If the kid is mine, then I'll become a packaged deal. It'll be us and you. I don't know if it's even fair to ask you to take on becoming a stepmother at eighteen years old, knowing you hate the kid's mother."

Tears welled up in her eyes again and she started sobbing. I pulled her into my hold, creating a fist with my right hand and massaging her neck with it while she boohooed. Skylar's sobs tugged at my heart strings, causing it to play a score of melancholy chords that saturated us. This was it. I could tell. This wasn't even our funeral; this was the wake. Look at us. Look at our remains. This was the end of Chance and Sky. Broderick and Skylar. The dreams of togetherness I had would be laid to rest today and thrown into the abyss. There was no way she was staying with me through this. A whole ass, real ass, breathing ass, living ass kid.

Chapter Four

SKYLAR

The pain from Chance's blow to my heart consumed me. The grief rocked me into a coma-induced state like melatonin. A guttural scream emitted from my mouth like a wild banshee. I was hurt. Injured. Gutted. I'd already been wounded by his betrayal, but this? This was too much to handle. A kid? And with her? There was no way I was sticking around for this type of embarrassment and drama. No way.

I'd cried so loud and for so long that I was exhausted. Blow after blow was thrown from my fists and landed on his person. That wasn't me. I'd never put hands on a man before. My mama always taught me not to do that.

"Not every man has an 'off' button. They weren't all raised to not hit women," she'd say. I'd usually take my 'L', curse, and cry; but today? Today I wanted to bite, kick, and scratch him. I became a dealer, dispensing blows to my pain pusher. I just wanted him to feel a tenth of the torment I was.

I don't know how or when it'd happened, but I tired myself out. Cried myself into a deep sleep. I don't know how long I was out; I just knew that when my eyes fluttered open, I was in my bed, lying on my back. I didn't even panic because I knew he was still there. I could smell and feel him. Focusing my eyes, I darted my eyeballs around the door and blinked rapidly. My orbs then found him on the bottom left corner of my bed—across from me. His body was hunched over. Elbows were locked onto his knees while his hands held his head that hung with gloom. I could feel his angst from here.

Startling him, I pulled back on my elbows and sat up in the bed with my back pressing against the headboard and pillows. The sound of my rousing drew his attention to me. He quickly looked at me then looked away. He probably didn't know what to say—Lord knows I didn't. Only the sounds of my ceiling fan coated my walls until he fully turned his body to face me. I felt him looking but I didn't want to give him my eyes. I knew I would burst into tears at any given moment. I'd almost wished he would've left me to cry in solace. So many thoughts were rummaging through my head. How could I stay on this campus to watch him play house with the next chick? I came to this school on my own recognizance, but with the full hopes of leaving this place engaged if not married to Zaïre in four years. Then, I come here and find out he's been cheating. It crushed me. I move on with Chance only to find out he's been aware of the deceit the entire time. And in the midst of all that, I get pregnant. I get rid of the baby and now he has a baby on the way with someone else. What the entire hell? Hell had to be playing tricks on me. I had to be under spiritual warfare or something because how else could I explain this?

"Sky..." he croaked out, interrupting my thoughts. His voice sounded tired, as if he had been sleeping, too; but he hadn't. I knew he hadn't because there was no way he could sleep in the same room with me without rapping his arms around me. That was us. Chance and Sky. The cuddles and feels. That kind of medicine would have soothed me—even if only for a second. Now we were worlds apart.

I lifted my brows to gesture "yes" because Lord knew I couldn't look at him.

"Baby..."

I shook my head 'no'. He couldn't talk his way into

my good graces after a kid—*especially after I just got rid of mine.* Guilt. Guilt, shame, and betrayal were the cycle playing in my mind. Wash. Rinse. And repeat. My hollowed stomach pained me at the mention of the world *baby.*

"You broke me," I whispered.

After a long pause, he replied, "I know."

"I won't let you do it again..." I stated, finally looking at him.

"I won't do it again," he paused, staring into my orbs. "I wish I could take it away. I don't even know if the baby is mine..."

"It is!" I shook, trying to force the words out. "I dreamt about your kids. It's yours. God showed me. I just didn't know what I was looking at. I thought I was trippn', but He was warning me. I think it's two."

He sighed, shaking his head. "I tried to tell myself it wasn't mine, but if you're saying god showed you, then it's real. I don't know god like that, but I know you do. I know that nigga be telling you shit." His face was solemn and crestfallen.

A dry chuckle escaped from my lips without my permission. *This nigga is a nuisance,* I thought to myself. He is so nescient to the world of Christianity and spirituality that he hadn't realized the error of his ebonics. Firstly, God is not a nigga, and you don't be cussing in the same sentence you mention Him in. It's wrong. You just don't do it. Out of respect and honor, the name of the Lord is to remain holy, but that's not how this guy speaks. In his own way, he was acknowledging Him in the only way he knew how. To him, He was the ultimate —a real ass nigga in a world of fakes. He couldn't reference God by using my lens, only through his own vantage point. He didn't know God like I did, but he knew me enough to hang on to my faith.

"Yeah... He does," was all I could say. Although my relationship with God didn't exactly mirror my parents', it was there. His presence was palpable in my life—even when I disregarded it for my own pleasures. I licked my dry, bottom lip. "A whole pregnancy though?"

Chance inched closer to me. "Shit's crazy. I thought that would be us..."

I instantly froze. He and I had never truly had a conversation about children before. We never had the time. "Wha... How do you know I want kids?" I frowned.

Chance sucked his teeth instantly in a non-believing manner. "You don't want to have my baby, Sky?" He said it as if the notion of that was the most preposterous thing he had ever heard me say. Like he just knew I was being difficult. Like our future children were written in the stars and I was illiterate.

My stomach and eyes folded inside my body where the guilt bubbled over. "We..well... that's obsolete nuh-now," I said in a lowly voice. Stuttering, I couldn't get my words together. He had no idea what I was copping to, but the idea of a child between us was quite literally as good as done.

"It doesn't have to be though," he raised his exasperated voice. "Baby, we can still work this out!"

"Work what out?" I asked, because I knew he wasn't expecting me to throw caution to the wind and be with his ready-made family.

"Us! You and me. We love each other. We can work through this," he loudly reasoned. "*I* want to work through this."

My face folded immediately in angst. No, it was more like anger. I was hurt and angered by this occurrence. "Chance, that sounds good in theory—well, good for you—but what about me? You want me to be a piece of your circle that you've already created with someone else? You want me to just sit idle as I watch you rub on her belly and her feet? And don't say you won't do that because you will. Whatever it takes to have a healthy baby, you will give."

"You want me to watch the kid, too? Maybe wipe its nose and help you open their Christmas gifts while simultaneously feeling like an outsider because I'm not an intricate link in this circle? You want to trap me with a baby that ain't even mine?"

"No!" Chance yelled. "I want you to stick to the damn plan! It's not like I cheated on you! I got her pregnant right before you, but that doesn't negate the love I have for you! She ain't my woman, that's just my kid!" He tried reasoning with me, but it wasn't working. "Or we at least presume she's having my kid." He paused to think, then shook the very thoughts from his head. "The point is, she don't mean shit to me; you do."

He hadn't done anything wrong, yet it cut so deep. I took a deep breath. "And you mean a lot to me as well." *Everything*. I wanted to say everything, but I wasn't ready to cop to that just yet. In just a short amount of time, we had gone from sworn enemies, to friends who became lovers, parents, and then this—whatever it was. "I'm not trying to punish you; I'm just trying to be realistic with me. I don't know how to deal with this level of ghetto," I blurted out. My words were laced with the purest form of contempt and haughtiness. Immediately, I wished I could vacuum my words right back in—I did not want to be offensive; it was just a gutter situation to me—but there was no other way to say.

Instead of being offended, Chance took a quick look at me, rolled onto his back, and bellowed out a great laugh. I mean, it was so hearty I felt the vibrations of his body on my end of the bed. It was hefty but lighthearted, and infectious. I giggled with him. Freely. His head was now adjacent to my feet, which were hidden under a blanket.

"I ain't mean to say it like *that*," I said. And I hadn't meant to. I meant what I said, but I didn't mean to come across so judgmental.

Chance kept laughing. His eyes rolled over to mine, and he hooted. "Nah, your saddity ass meant exactly what you said."

I lifted my right leg from under the blanket and kicked his shoulder lightly. "Whatever, nigga. Well, maybe I did because y'all ghetto as hell," I rolled my eyes. "Y'all are always talking about me for being uppity, but I own it. You don't own yours."

"Don't own what?" Amusement danced in his eyes. "You're saying *I'm* stuck up?"

I scoffed and rolled my eyes. "It's cloaked behind all this macho bravado, but you are hella bougie, sir."

"How?" Chance sat up on his elbow and faced me. How we had gone from screaming and hollering to this was beyond me.

My face folded in disbelief. "What kind of luggage do you have, Mr. Sinclair?"

"Whatever man," he waved me off. "I like nice things."

"You're aristocratic. You have Louis Vuitton bags, luxury sheets...your jeans are even from luxury brands.

You booked a private Disney tour for us after hours, which I know set you back a pretty penny. Your family is one of the most notorious families in the underworld of Chicago—that right there comes with a set of privileges few people will ever see in their lifetime. And you dated me. That lets you know everything you needed to know right there. You're not around the way Chance no more, and you haven't been for a very long time."

Chance shrugged and resumed his position on his back, eyes still on me. "Aye, you remember when you came to your first Omega party?"

"Yes," I closed my eyes and folded my arms over my breasts. "It was so lit in there."

Chance shook his head while removing the blanket cover from my feet without permission. "I was miserable the whole time," he vented while pulling my feet on his chest. He began to massage the right one right in the arch part. It felt so good I almost forgot to speak.

"Why?" It came out like a groan though it wasn't intended to. It just felt good to be touched. It had been four, tough weeks without his magical hands and I missed them.

"'Cause yo' hot ass came in there with no clothes on," he squeezed my foot and shot me a look of angst.

"I had on clothes," I stuck my tongue out at him.

"A thong ain't no clothes, nigga," Chance laughed

and moved on to my left foot. "I wanted to beat Zaïre's ass for dancing on you."

I shrugged. "I wasn't paying him any attention. My eyes were squarely on you." I sighed. "You were dancing real nasty on your baby mama though." I tried to kick him, as I felt myself becoming triggered.

Chance caught my foot before I could kick him and kissed my big toe. "Who did I end my night with though?"

I sat back with tears staining my eyes. "Me."

"Dead ass." That New York swagger emitted from his pores. He bobbed his head up and down, continuing his caress of my feet. It felt so good, the massage was sending shock waves up to my heart. "You belonged to someone else; I never belonged to her; we just had a good time..."

"That's going to last a lifetime," I added, bringing up the baby.

He shook his head. "I guess so..."

I wiggled my feet away from his grasp.

"I always want to end my nights with you," he confessed. "All of them. Since Disney. Seeing that wedding shit made me want that with you. I want us to be like my OG and Grand. 'Til death do us part type shit."

I shook my head. "I want that, too, but seeing you have a family with her? That's out." I sighed. "I can't do this one with you. I can't share pieces of you with Nicci Gilbert."

Chance chuckled lowly at the jab I threw. His alarm sounded on his phone, startling both of us. "I got to go." He sat up and stared at the blank wall ahead. He was stalling. I was stalling.

"The right love at the wrong time, I guess," I sighed and combed my fingers through my dry hair.

"I'm honored to experience that shit. Our love story ain't dead," he decreed.

"I can't take seeing you," I blurted out. "Like, you can't pop up, we can't hang out, we can't kick it. I need the distance." I could never return to just being his friend. I loved him so much my heart was already tender and ticking like a bomb. Watching him move on with another family would make it explode.

"If you won't let me in now, I can only pray god has mercy enough on a nigga to let me in heaven, 'cause I know yo' ass is getting in." He chuckled. "I hope I get a buddy pass or some shit so I can be with you in the afterlife and beyond." He paused. "But I might get kicked out because the minute one of them angels look at you too long, I'm going to pluck Gabriel's fucking wings, and be sent to hell."

My eyes coated with water. "That's the sweetest thing you've ever said to me."

"I meant that shit, too." He was so ghetto. So New York. So mine.

Chance stood up from the bed. He pulled up his pants and planted a kiss on my forehead. "Take care, Shorty."

I nodded. "Goodnight, Broderick," I said as a tear escaped my eyes. No more Chance and Sky.

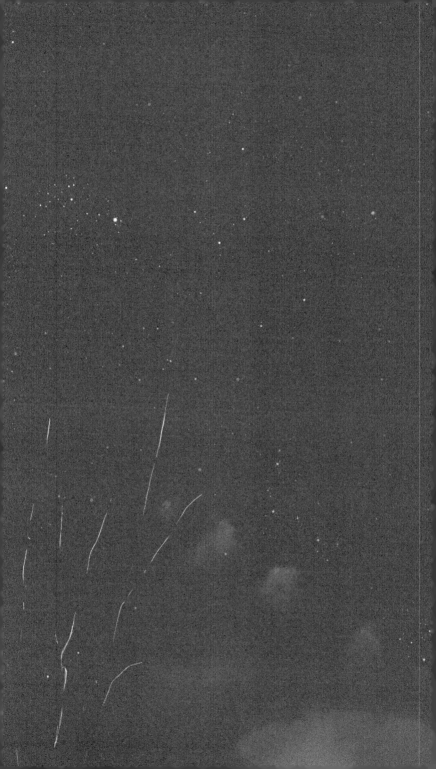

Chapter Five

SKYLAR

> Me:
>
> 911 emergency! Reconnect the community!

I finally hit Kecia's line after sitting in my room for three days. It was a line from this old show that me and my mama used to watch reruns of all the time. She made me sit down and binge watch the series with her my junior year of high school. That's what made me want to attend an HBCU. I could identify with most of the characters, but Lena and Dorian were my favorites. However, my first-year collegiate experience ended up mirroring Charmaine and Lance. Charmaine just knew she was coming into her first year of college being couple goals, but baby, the second Lance hit that campus and saw all those beautiful women, he forgot all the promises he ever made her and chased tail. Now ain't that some mess?

For three days I secluded myself from the world. Chance had been gone for that long, and I just sat in my room, marinating in darkness. I had not paid much attention to my hygiene, my hair, nor my nourishment, which was so unlike me. I couldn't even pick myself up enough to go to class. Instead, I'd been swimming in the black hole of despair. This abyss of depression seemed never-ending. I was calling myself fasting. It was the only way I knew how to cleanse my spirit. I'd seen my parents fast and get results. I'd fasted with my church and even my family. My dad would always quote the scripture when Jesus said, "This kind only goes out through prayer and fasting." The quote derives from a story when the disciples were trying to free this demon-possessed kid. They warred with him all day, but the kid was still possessed. When Jesus showed up, the parents ran to tell on the disciples. They had brought their kid to them thinking the same healing sauce Jesus had would be on his pupils and they would be able to get the job done. Well, they were wrong. With as much power as the disciples had, they were unable to triage the accurate prescription that would be needed for the kid's freedom. Jesus then taught the disciples this valuable lesson. Some things don't require a lot of noise—but self-denial.

Fasting is a tool my family and church lives by, but I'm guessing I did it wrong. I went on a three-day, self-imposed fast. I asked God to take the feelings I had for Chance away. I begged. I hadn't answered any phone calls. I didn't want to talk. I sent out generic texts so my parents, siblings, and friends would know I was alive. Other than that, my voice and pain had been muted. Just silent prayers and pleas reaching up towards the heavens. The only sounds ricocheting in this room were my fan and the soundtrack of my hunger pangs. I only got up to relieve myself in the restroom. That's it.

Today, I decided to speak to my friend at least. I had given darkness three entire days of my life, and still no light showed up. If I did not have any human connection soon, I was sure to lose what was left of my mind. *Maybe God isn't speaking to me because of the abortion,* I thought. I still had the sadness looming over me because of my greatest sin. That had to be the reason. Because why else would God not do what I asked when I denied myself before Him. Literally, fasting was always the *get it quick* regimen at church. Why wasn't my deliverance from this fine ass man taking place? Why was God virtually ignoring my supplication? It's very much giving "Why has Thou forsaken me" vibes and I'on like it!

My stomach was twisted in knots. Grief was no joke. The shit was a tricky emotion. How was it remotely possible for me to grieve a child I hadn't wanted just days

73

prior? I detested the very existence of the thing, now somehow, I am riddled with guilt, shame, and overwhelming grief of *my* child. I was mourning the two losses, which all felt the same. I didn't know what hurt worse—the relationship or the seed—regardless, I was torn up. My heart felt like it was bleeding out. And I needed it to stop. I wanted it to stop. But there was no end in my immediate sight.

Kecia texted be back.

I'm on my way.

I wet my pallet and used it to moisturize my crusty ass lips. Peeling my naked self from my bed, I got up and went to the restroom. Pondering my sadness, I wallowed in my bed, holding my pee until I could no longer stand it. I held it for so long, my right leg was starting to feel a little funny. I went to the restroom, relieved myself, and brushed my teeth. I played H.E.R.'s "Come Through" while straightening up.

Almost missed my flight today
I look good even though I feel shitty
I just got back out this way
You already got plans for the city
Call 'em off, could you call 'em off for me?
You're always goin' on and on

Got it all, ask me why I'll never leave
I don't go out much
But you should come through tonight
I'm chillin' on the Westside, boo
Call my homegirl, tell your best friend he could slide too
On the low, a remote location
I don't want them seein' me gettin' faded
You should come through tonight
I only kick it with a tight crew
They won't tell 'cause they tryna live they best life too
On the low, on my own, I'll be wavy
Hit me on my phone, I'll be waitin'
Yeah, yeah

I didn't have time to take the shower I knew I desperately needed. I barely had the energy to do it. After washing my hands, my feet shuffled back to my bedroom so I could at least put on a night gown.

I dug into my drawer and extracted a white t-shirt. Recognizing it immediately, a tear began to trickle down the right side of my face. It was Chance's, of course. One of his Gucci tees. I loved to wear his shirts. They'd drown my smaller frame, but they smelled like him. Every time I wore one, I felt cocooned in his love. Not to mention the fact that Chance *loved* to see me in one of his shirts and a bonnet, frolicking around either of our apartments. *It was...* I shook off the thoughts of the past and stuffed the shirt in the back of the drawer and grabbed a robe. That was the safest thing I could put on. I didn't need to be triggered by the threads I was barely hanging on to.

Lookin' at you cry, goin' crazy
If I could, I would take the pain away
I don't see that smile I made
You already made plans that ain't with me
Tryin' hard, I been tryin' hard to breathe
Inhale, exhale, you expel what you been doin' to me
Fightin' it off, you been fightin' me off for weeks
Don't leave 'cause I need ya
But you should come through tonight
I'm chillin' on the Westside, boo
Call my homegirl, tell your best friend he could slide too
On the low, a remote location
I don't want them seein' me gettin' faded
You should come through tonight (yeah)
I only kick it with a tight crew (yeah, ay)
They won't tell 'cause they tryna live they best life too (no)
On the low, on my own, I'll be wavy (yeah)
Hit me on my phone, I'll be waitin'
Yeah, yeah

While I tied my gray, terry cloth robe around my waist, I heard the doorbell ring. I toed into my black, furry Ugg slippers and ambled to the door. Looking through the peep hole, I verified my guest, and opened up.

"Oh, hell naw!" Kecia walked in and tooted her nose up at me. "You smell like day old cabbage, girl."

I shook my head, embarrassed. "I—" Tears immediately poured from my eyes. I cupped my face with my hands and audibly cried. Like, I wept.

"You're sad and it's okay to be sad. Do I need to call Chance over?" She awkwardly tapped her shaking fingers against my back as I shook my head to gesture 'no'. "Okay, girl, well what do you want me to do because I'm not the best at comforting hoes. I've been trying my best all week, but all these tears is getting weird now."

I pulled my head up and chuckled deeply. "You stupid." I wiped the tears from my eyes, while silently promising myself that they would be my last. "Nah, don't call Chance. I don't want to speak to that nigga." I gulped.

"Huh?" Kecia asked, confused. "Don't tell me you told him, and he cut up on you!" She hypothesized about the abortion.

"Oh, nah!" My eyes bucked. "That's pretty much going to the grave with me." I smirked, faintly to downplay the seriousness of that thought. No one could ever know about the procedure, and I was praying to God I could trust this chick with that vital piece of information. I prayed that she would never turn on me like the likes of Sage. If she ever did, I would deny that shit so badly she would seem like a psychotic mental patient by the time I was done dragging her through the mud. It would be 'screw her' to protect me. Life was becoming a colossal game of Survivor, and I was determined to remain on the island. "But we did break up," I admitted. "I haven't eaten anything in three days. I just want to get this nigga out of my system and move on."

Kecia released an exasperated breath. "Oh, if only love worked that way." She shook her head. "You should get dressed though. I'm taking you out and making you feel better." Kecia crossed her arms over her chest as if her word were final and I was actually going to go out with her.

And that's when I finally paid attention to her outfit. Kecia donned a nude-colored mini dress. The mocked neck, short-sleeved number had asymmetrical, diagonal drawstring detailing going from her hip bone to her thigh, causing a ruching effect that made the dress. Her feet worked some clear heels, while her hair was pulled back into a donut at the back of her head, causing attention to fall to her slightly large ears that were adorned with gold hoop earrings. Her light beat and pale pink lip gloss topped the look off.

"Where the heck are you going?" I pondered while looking her up and down. "You look pretty."

"Why thank you," Kecia said while twirling around,

prancing like she was the second coming of Kenya Moore. "Anyway, we're going up to Onyx for open mic night. Everyone's wearing nude. Go, get dressed, and let's go." She said that and sauntered over to my couch to cop a squat like she was waiting on me to leave.

"First of all, negro, I am not twenty-one so I can't get in Onyx. It's a whole lounge. Secondly, I'm not going anywhere." I adjusted my robe to close it a bit tighter. "My itinerary for tonight entails sulking, pining, and pondering over how stupid it was for me to fall in love with that nigga in two point five seconds. I am not leaving this apartment, let alone singing in front of strangers—if I was able to get in."

"Pish posh," Kecia waved me off. "You can sulk tomorrow. Tonight, I think you should get dressed and focus on having a good time. My boy, Fat Tony, is part owner and he's going to let you in. So, shower and get dressed. You look a mess. Chop, chop, heifer. There's always ballers, music execs, bosses, and niggas with bank rolls in Onyx."

My head drew back in mock offense. "Girl, why do you even know someone named Fat Tony?"

She shrugged. "His name was Fat Tony when I met him. He's an Italian kid I've known since fifth grade. That's how he got the name. Italians and their nicknames," she chuckled. "He and his wife, Yadira—she's Black—are the owners."

"Good to know," I shrugged, then plopped down in one of the chairs I had in the living room. "Enjoy because I'm not going."

Kecia shook her head at me. "Little girl, the best way to get over a nigga ain't pining, it's living. You know I know. I wish I would've had a friend like me to tell me to get my snotty nose ass outside and paint the town pink when my ex broke my heart. Instead, I cried and replayed the memories in my head, pulling me back into an abyss of darkness and sorrow. The nigga abused me twice—once in the relationship and again in my memories. I'm telling you right now, do not stop living because your heart hurts. Let that nigga know you ain't languishing because y'all are through. Post selfies. Thirst trap. Transfer that pain from you to his chocolate ass. Get you a new nigga. Something!"

My ears perked at the thought of Chance being upset for seeing me out and about—looking alive. The thought of this hard, nefarious nigga becoming weakened by the semblance of fun I was falsely indulging in intrigued me. His life was being altered by the presence of an incoming kid, but mine didn't have to stop. Although I was weakened by his absence, the thought of gut punching him for what his and his basic baby mama's actions had done to us was interesting. Childish, but interesting.

After mulling over her sentiments, I decided to get

up and go. "I guess I'll tag along," I murmured, down-playing my excitement. Chance and I followed one another on all social media platforms. I knew he would see me, and I could not wait.

Onyx was only a stone's throw away from campus. I needed music to get ready. Something upbeat to get me into a better mood. Something to cause me to switch my mind focusing on the hollow pit in my belly to turning myself into the baddie that was dwelling within. I turned on Pardison Fontaine's "Backin' It Up"—the version with all the cussing—to get into the mood.

Ahhh

Cardi!

Turn around, f*ck it all the way up

Bust it down, turn around, f*ck it all the way up

Bust it down, turn around, f*ck it—look

Let's get it straight, girl, you don't need a nigga for nothin'

Lookin' better every day, you got that Benjamin Button

Claimin' he don't got a girl, you know niggas be frontin'

You don't need no b*tch comin' up to you as a woman (ayy)

And you a boss, so you hate when niggas waste time (ayy)

You too pretty to be paused on the FaceTime (ayy)

MY CALF LENGTH BOX BRAIDS WERE COLORED chocolate brown, and I decided to match my fit and makeup to my skin. I was a chocolate fountain dripping good luck and Hershey's kisses. I put on a sheer, brown turtleneck with Fendi f's all over it. You could see through the top to my soul; so, I put on a brown bralette that made my boobs look fuller than they actually were. I paired it with brown, high waist, faux leather leggings and brown monogrammed Fendi boots.

Throw that shit over here, girl, that's what it's for (what you say?)
You know how to go and get a bag, don't you? (Ayy)
You know how to make a bitch mad, don't you (Ayy)
Make your ex wanna get it back, that's a fact
Say it louder for the bitches in the back (Ayy)
I know how to go and get a bag, don't I (don't I)
I know how to get a bitch mad, don't I (yeah)
Make my ex wanna get it back, that's a fact
Say it louder for the bitches in the back (ayy)
Back, back-backin' it up
I'm the queen of talkin' shit, then I'm backin' it up (yeah)
Back, back-backin' it up
Throw that money over here, nigga,
That's what it's for (what you say?)

I did a neutral make up look with a matte, chocolate lip and twenty-five millimeter lashes. I accessorized with a crossbody Fendi bag and a gold watch. I was ready to go in an hour and a half—record timing for me. I usually needed about three hours to fully prepare to go out.

"I'm ready!" I spooked Kecia with my loud tone. She was sitting on my couch with one of my Love Belvin books in her hands. She was my favorite author of all time.

"Sheeeeeit! I just got to chapter three. This Ezra dude sounds sterile as hell. You look great though! Pop out, girl!" Kecia sing songed.

"Thaaaaanks!" I sang back. "But you have no idea. That Pastor Ezra Carmichael is my current book boyfriend! He's anything but boring," I waved her off and turned to my alarm system. Chance had installed it when we came back from Disney.

"Girl, what the heck is a book boyfriend?" Kecia asked, none the wiser.

I rolled my eyes at her inability to read the context clues. Lifting my eyes to the skies, I thought about the best way to articulate my mental fixation. "Book boyfriends are the niggas whose arms you run into when your real man ain't acting right. You get lost in their hold, their alpha, their swag. Though they are someone else's brainchild, book boyfriends give you hope that real niggas are somewhere out there." I shrugged. "The best boyfriends are fictional boyfriends. You can only pray that they're based on real boyfriends, you know?" In this moment, I wish life was as simple as a book. At least in the books I read, you know the characters are going to get back together. With me, love had been stifled.

"Dang," Kecia whispered. "You weird as hell for being that passionate about a dude that's on paper. I almost thought you were talking about a real man." She jested.

"Girl, don't knock it until you delve into the world of fiction." I smiled brightly. "We need to start a book club or something so I can put you on!" I flipped the light switch. I looked back at her and said, "Let's go."

Kecia drove us to Onyx, which was only seven minutes from campus. When we pulled up, valet was immediately at our doors, opening them kindly. They were so nice and accommodating. I was used to this princess treatment because I was Bishop Lawson's daughter, so I felt at ease. We walked up to the doors of the lounge. I could tell just from the outside that it was upscale, not some hole in the wall. I had heard of upper-classmen talking about this place, but I was getting ready to have the Onyx experience.

"Fat Tonyyyyyy!" Kecia sang out. She had a habit of doing that.

"Keke! What up, girl!" He bear-hugged her. Fat Tony was fine as heck. He was a tall, Italian heartthrob. He had some extra weight on him, but that took nothing away from his boyish face or that thick, Italian American accent. He sounded to be second or third generation American. "You hangin' it with us tonight, doll?"

"Yeah, me and my girl, Sky, here," she pointed at me while he put a wristband on her right wrist.

"Hey ya, Girl Sky!" He waved me over. "She's gorgeous, Keeks." He winked his fine, fat eye at me, and I immediately swooned.

"Hey! I only roll with the best," Kecia shrugged. "Come on, Sky," she waved me over to them so he could put a band on my wrist as well.

"Thank you, handsome," I complimented him back.

"Ah! Don't gas me, darlin'" he said as he planted a kiss on the back of my hand and tapped it twice. "Entry's on me! Head straight up to the VIP. Enjoy yourselves."

"Ah, Tony, I could have sat on the floor. You spoil me!" Kecia flirted as we walked inside.

"I thought you said that man had a wife," I pondered aloud behind her.

"He got a wife and he's a flirt," she shrugged. "My flirting bought us VIP entry." We bobbed and weaved in between people in line as we headed upstairs to a VIP lounge. The entire interior was decorated in black and gold. It looked expensive as hell, and I felt my weight in gold with each step I took.

Kecia took my hand in hers so we wouldn't get separated by the crowd. "Now, just be cool when we get up here," she whispered. "The VIP is always filled with influencers and hustlers, pills and potions, that a church girl like you ain't used to."

My face folded. I had been sneaking out the house since sixteen. I had seen some things with my own two eyes. "Girl, I'm grown. I've been to clubs before."

Kecia scoffed. "Maybe. But you ain't been to Onyx's VIP section. This is for niggas that hit the hustler's lotto and bitches that want to be on their radar."

Before I could respond, we were at the door. Kecia knocked three times, and the door opened. I clutched my pocketbook. Everything in the section was immaculate. The carpet was red, sofas were gold, and there were different gold frames and mirrors adorning the walls. Everything was stellar. Everything looked like money. And the people matched. Most of them were men. Mostly Black. They were all drinking, engaging, or smoking. Each of them gave us a glance as we walked by. They all looked as if they were sizing us up, wondering who I was and why I was here. I intentionally put a little more stank in my walk to instigate their intrigue.

In the distance, I could hear a singer crooning to Chanté Moore's "It's Alright."

Hello my love,
Before the sun rises, after it goes down,
I love ya, I love ya,
I say it over and over again,

I love ya, hey, hey, hey.
Relax your mind, we can be free together,
Take our time, even through the tears,
I'm staying right here, I'm waiting right here,
Oh, we're going through some hard times,
But it will be, alright.

The young lady was singing her behind off. She hardly sounded amateur as Kecia led me to a sofa. We took our seats and I continued to take in the place.

"You want a drink?" she asked.

I looked around. "Yeah, should we go to the bar or —" Before I could finish my question, a scantily clad woman came up and took our order.

"Welcome to Onyx, sexy mamas. What can I get y'all. I got whatever you can dream of to tickle your fancy." The redbone with dimples and a bald head winked at me. Her voice sounded like that of a snake charmer. Enticing and intrinsic. Her eyes were seductive and sultry. Like, I knew I was a straight up, heterosexual woman, but her gaze had me questioning everything. The heifer was sucking me into a web of need and seduction. Her right brow went up knowingly.

"Hey, girl," Kecia spoke up, breaking our eye contact, therefore this waitress's hypnosis.

"Kecia?" The young lady got excited and hugged my friend. "Girl, how've you been?"

"I'm good," Kecia said, letting go of their embrace. "This is my friend's first time here. We're taking it light tonight." She winked.

What does that mean?, I thought to myself.

"Light?" The waitress' face folded as her eyes gave me the once over, then went back to my companion for the night. "So, no rice crispy treats and brownies? The *uge?*" (The word was short for 'usual.')

Kecia smiled and nodded. "Maybe just the brownies. She just wants a drink though."

"Who the hell eats rice crispy treats and brownies together?" I frowned. "Sounds like a stomachache in the making." The waitress perked up and faced me.

"Oh!" She quizzically eyed Kecia.

"She's a square, Amber," Kecia winked.

"A what?" I asked, offended.

"Meaning a newbie," Kecia tried to ease the blow.

"You had already said tha—"

"Oh! Why didn't you just say that?" she asked Kecia, interrupting me. "Well, in that case, what are you drinking? I can recommend our Pucker Up. It's a frozen drink that'll surely have you on your ass tonight." She winked. "Or, if you're planning on singing, you might get the Liquid Courage." The girl shimmied.

Something fishy was happening. They were in on some kind of secret that I wanted in on.

"Um... Do y'all have buffalo wings?" I asked,

wondering if it were a stupid question. "You didn't give me a menu, so I don't really know what to choose from."

"Oh, girl. That's because our VIPs don't really order from the menu. It's more like a 'your wish is my command' type of thing." Amber, whose name I just learned, clued me in.

I frowned. "If that's the case, then I want a lobster roll and a Liquid Courage."

"Coming right up!" She and her titties bounced away, leaving me confused. "Oh!" She turned around to face me. "I'll put your name on the list to perform."

"You want to take your pictures now?" Kecia asked with her hand extended, waiting for my phone. Like she just knew the answer was 'yes'.

"I swear tonight is moving in fast forward. I was just in my apartment crying, now you got me outside and about to sing in front of a bunch of people," I shook my head. The whole night seemed to be moving swiftly after three nights of non-movement. I glided out of my seat and found myself a spot in the corner of the room to pose for my photos. With my hands on my hips, I poked my chest in and out, swiveling my head around for the best angels while Kecia counted to three and cheered me on.

"It's giving face!" she pumped me up.

I lifted my right arm and placed it over my head, while sticking my tongue out to capacity. It was a bad ass pose. Instantly, I knew that was my shot—the money shot. "Ok, that's it," I giggled and said to Kecia.

Taking my phone away from her, I posted the photo on all my social media pages with the caption, "If I'm too much, go find less. I'll even send you some referrals." Of course, Chance was the inspiration behind it. Pleased with myself, I went back over to our table. "Girl, I don't know how I let you talk me into singing. I only sing at church for real." I chuckled, feeling the nervous energy coming over me.

"Honey, I *wish* I could sing. I would be right up there with you; but I think it'll be a good step in the right direction." She shrugged. "I just wanted to get you out the house. You need a break from sobbing."

I nodded. "You're right!" I yelled over the loud music. "Heck, I'm surprised I have any tears left." I glanced around the room, feeling myself growing more emotional.

"You're a person with feelings. The breakup *just* happened," Kecia shrugged with her face. "Of course, you're upset, but tonight, we let loose." She stood up and whirled her body around in a sexy circle, dancing to the beat of the song that was playing.

I giggled at her goofiness and scanned the room with my eyes. Three tables up from us, a gentleman was separating a white, powdery substance. I couldn't hold the shock from my face. "Trick is that co—"

"See? A Square." Kecia shook her head. "Powerful men dabble. It's a party drug," she shrugged.

My mien folded. "I've been around powerful men my whole life. Ain't na'an one of them been no crack-head," I whispered.

Laughter flew from Kecia's mouth so quickly, she had to hang on to her seat. The laugh was guttural, and so loud that other occupants in our space turned around to look at us. She was doing the full-blown, Black folks-cackle-with-their-whole-bodies kind of laugh. I didn't understand why. I was flabbergasted.

"Fool," she said as her shoulders continued to bounce up and down in her fit of funny. "Girl, that is not crack. Coke and crack are two different things. Crack is cheap."

"Oh," my brows flew up into my hairline. Here I was learning yet another thing about "the world". You never know how sheltered you are until you meet other people. I tucked my full lips inside my mouth, feeling stupid.

Kecia sighed away her last fits of laughter. "Girl, that was funny. Here comes our stuff."

The brown sugar colored Onyx model of a waitress sauntered over with a tray of food and drinks belonging to us.

"Here's your special treats," she winked at Kecia.

"Thanks, babes," Kecia said, and went right in for her brownie. "Mmm... Good."

"Only the best for you, doll." Amber smiled and turned her attention to me. "Here's your Liquid Courage and lobster roll with French fries. You might want to get a few swallows of that drink in because there's only one other person in line before you." She pointed to the screen with all the performer's names in order.

"Shit," I cursed. Grabbing my food, I took a bite of the sandwich, which was seasoned to perfection. "Mmm... Lord, forgive me for not praying. Thank You!" I took a few sips of my drink. It was a gold margarita sitting on dry ice, which made smoke emit from it. I danced in my seat as the liquid dripped down my throat. It was sweet and sour at the same time. I immediately tasted the alcohol and relished in the feeling it gave. I didn't even care about the stares coming from Kecia and Amber. This was my first meal in days. I hadn't realized how starved I was. "You gonna eat that?" I asked Kecia while turbo-chomping on my lobster roll.

She eyed me quizzically. "Girl, it's an edible. I didn't know you liked these."

My mouth formed a silent 'o' as I passed on what I thought would be desert. I had only tried smoking twice: once with Zaïre and the other time with the twins. Emphasis on the word tried. I hadn't known Kecia long enough to feel comfortable enough to be out of my mind around her just yet. I could only see myself doing that with Chance. Well, that was before...

"You ready?" Amber asked, interrupting my thoughts as I tossed four fries to the back of my mouth.

"Mmm hmm..." I sing-songed and took a final gulp of my drink. I wanted to drink as much as possible before I left my seat. There was no way I would be picking that glass up again after it was out of my sight. "Wish me luck," I said over my shoulder to Kecia as I followed our waitress out of the section. I immediately felt the rush of the liquor surging through my system.

"Knock 'em dead! Just have fun, church girl," Kecia replied.

Amber took me by the hand as we maneuvered through the crowd of people. Her velvety touch was a clear contrast to my misted palms. "What are you singing?"

I tucked my bottom lip into my mouth and replied, "Something from my heart..."

"Alright, ladies and gentlemen!" The MC said, "Give it up for Flyy Skyy." That was the name I put on the list.

I combed my fingers through my braided inches and ambled over to the microphone. I touched the mic stand like I had never seen one of them before.

"Y'all got to excuse me," I emoted. "I usually only sing at church so I'm real nervous; but I decided to sing this Jazmine Sullivan song because the song is legendary and because it's how I feel." I cleared my throat.

"You got it, girl," a lady from the audience called out, making me smile.

"Y'all can play the record," I said as I rubbed misted palms to my shaking thighs. I took a deep breath and closed my eyes as I heard the sounds of the piano playing.

I had high hopes for us baby
Like I was on dope for us baby
Chasin' after a high that I'll never get back again
So we turn into three long years
And it became painfully clear that we
We would never see those days again
But I guess forever, doesn't last too long forever
Doesn't last too long forever
Doesn't last too long forever these days, hey
And I try to believe that we could make it
But trying don't work, so I just have to face that forever
Doesn't last too long forever these days, hey

I placed my index fingers on my ears so I could fully hear myself. My voice shook as violently as my thighs. I took a deep breath to calm my nerves. There was no way I was going to fumble "Forever Doesn't Last" in front of all these people.

Still think about the good times we had
And how you used to make me laugh
But baby I know most times we were meant to revolve
So every time I wanna call, baby what always helps
Is when I think of the pain, and realize
I'm better off by myself

As I sang, I imagined the day I met Chance.

"*Before I could pull my eyes from my cell and focus them on what was in front of me, I nose dove straight into a man's chest. His muscular chest. I was so frazzled I didn't even care to look up into his eyes. My right hand went straight to the aching soreness of my nose. I cupped it then looked down at my palm, inspecting it for blood and damage. I'd always been labeled as a pretty girl. My face was one of my most valued commodities. I was pissed the hell off that something, anything, could have marred my face. I'd been in my own world, checking my phone, not paying attention to anyone around me, and then thwap! My chest heaved up and down. I hadn't even allowed my face to glance back up but felt hundreds of eyes gawking my way.*

95

And this chest with legs had interrupted the flow of College Lane.

"So, Shorty, you not gon' say excuse me or nothing? Damn!"

The meanness of his firm growl caused my head to jerk back. The thick, New York accent and the rasp of his vocal cords annoyed the hell out of me. The tone he had taken with me, his naturally authoritative timbre, took me aback. People normally walked on eggshells around me. I was always treated with kid gloves, like a princess. Church royalty. It wasn't until I came here that people didn't know who I was. Before today, I'd always been the big fish in the small pond. My last name rang bells. Most people around the Chicagoland area either knew of me or my family, but this nigga was speaking to me like I was scum. Sure, I should have been paying attention to where I was going; and, yes, I should apologize, but who the hell was he talking to?

Finally, my slanted eyes scrolled up to meet his. They were brown. Brown and basic. They looked sleepy as hell. I rolled my head up then down, evaluating the imagery before me. He looked like a typical New Yorker. Ripped blue jeans, sky blue Dior t-shirt, sky blue underwear, and wheat-colored Timberland boots. He had style. About four chains rested around his neck. *I know this nigga's feet musty as hell in them boots. It ain't hot enough to be wearing them,* I thought to herself. But even if I wanted to be impressed by his Dior drip, full lips, the scowl on his face, dimples, chocolate skin, or the goatee, I couldn't be because his attitude had pissed me off to the highest level of pisstivity.

"Excuse me?" my head drew back.

"Yo' lil ass rude as shit. Watch where you going, Shorty. You done got makeup and shit all on my shirt. The hell?" He grimaced and inspected his expensive t-shirt.

"And didn't even say sorry! Ugh! They just letting anybody in D.U. now." The groupie on his arm rolled her eyes and chimed in.

"Nigga, I was about to say sorry for running into your ignorant ass, but you didn't give me a chance to. But it wasn't that deep for you to be talking all crazy in my face. And secondly, I don't know you, prosti-thot, so keep it cute when you address me," my ego interjected, responding to the guy and his groupie.

"You need to stop shaking your big ass bobblehead around like that before that shit fall off. Now, say you're sorry. I got shit to do," he announced as if I would care or cower to his larger-than-life presence. I didn't know who he was, but judging by the amount of people who stopped moving when he did, I would say he was pretty popular. I didn't care though. No one would punk Skylar Lawson. I would have offered him a gracious apology had he not tried to make a spectacle of me; but now, the joke would be on him. I looked him up and down and smirked.

"I'm sorry... that your mother didn't raise you better. You're giving Q from Moesha, but you're about twenty years too late. Now, if you'll excuse me, I got stuff to do. Be blessed." With that, I took off, walking back to my apartment with an aching nose and heart. I felt him looking back at me as I walked off. I audibly heard him say, *"Females,"* but didn't care. *"Freshmen females at that. She had to be a freshman because only freshmen came on campus dressed like a D.U. mascot."* I ignored his words to the groupies that surrounded him. Mascot? I mean, I was rocking Davis University joggers, a t-shirt, and even the socks, but

am I not supposed to? My slides and purse are
Louis Vuitton though; so, I shouldn't look too
bad, I thought to myself.

A tear fell from my eye as I remembered our begin-
nings. He was rude from that day to this one—and so
was I. But his antics caused my heart to flutter and my
Good Girl to take notice. He weakened me. I was trying
my hardest to find strength in our wake, but Lord knows
I was feeble.

> *'Cause forever, doesn't last too long forever*
> *Doesn't last too long forever*
> *Doesn't last too long forever these days, hey*
> *And I try to believe that we could make it*
> *But trying don't work, so I just have to face that forever*
> *Doesn't last too long forever these days, hey*

Our love literally made no sense on paper, but as sure
as I swayed my hips to the beat, I knew it had existed. It
was true. It was palpable. But it was also gone. I was silly
for pursuing it, especially after he answered my phone
call while in bed with his now baby mama. I should have
acted like we never were, but I had to win. I had to have
him—even though I had someone else. I had to love him.

 "Yerr," Chance answered.

"What it do? Where you at?" I could hear faint noise in the background.

"Ain't shit. What's up? You need me?"

"I know yo' ass is lyin'!" I heard Nicole say in the background. It was ridiculously loud and purposely so. She wanted me to hear her. She wanted the smoke.

"Man, chill out!" Chance warned.

I giggled, though hurt. "Don't holler at her. You should've told me you were busy. I was just calling to tell you that I'd cooked, but it's cool. Enjoy Nikki Richie."

"How the hell are you tight with what you got going on?" Chance asked, referring to my boyfriend.

"Who's upset, Broderick?" I shot. "I'm good. Enjoy your lady. Talk later." I hung up. Hurt. I was hurt and in a whole relationship.

My breath hitched as my belly quivered. A wave of heat hit my body as I sang. My chest heaved involuntarily as my body began to react. I was no longer nervous, I had peace and strength. I literally felt a jolt of electricity zap up my spine and through my chest. My palms dried and my curved spine straightened. It must've been the Liquid Courage kicking in. I flickered my eyes open, now equipped with the confidence to do so. Suddenly, I looked up as I continued to croon.

Lord knows I gave it my all
I couldn't save us from falling
Cause some people aren't meant to be together forever

Our eyes immediately connected as they walked through the VIP section. It wasn't Liquid Courage that had given me confidence. A certain leggy, brute, slanted-eyed athlete had just walked in with a few insignificant others. His brown, angry orbs were stapled to mine. He was shooting mad daggers through my soul. I took a deep breath. I wanted to run away. I didn't want him to hear my singing shit about his love that he had to share with some pie-faced chick and their ugly ass son. Okay, that was mean, but I was feeling mean. I wanted to scratch his cornea for breaking us up. But I couldn't. I had to suck it up. I could not pretend like the tears hadn't fallen from my eyes. The song was almost over. I had to wipe my eyes and perform. I wasn't carrying this pain back to my room. I was going to leave it all here on the stage. I looked at him intently and began to sing.

'Cause forever, doesn't last too long forever
Doesn't last too long forever
Doesn't last too long forever these days, hey

And I try to believe that we could make it
But trying don't work, so I just have to face that forever
Doesn't last too long forever these days

I patted my hands against my chest. The crowd began to cheer as I sang to my ex. He was on the floor higher than me, sitting down cocky as hell. The only one not wearing a shade of brown, he rocked a full denim fit. His legs were wide, one extending past the other. His face was expressionless, but I knew he caught the vibes.

There were many others in the building, yet none of them existed. I was sick of being weak for this nigga. I thought I'd loved Zy, but the feelings I felt for him paled in comparison to the ache in my heart Chance had created.

Chance bit down on his bottom lip as I took a deep breath and finished the song. I could see Amber taking orders for everyone at the table, but his eyes were glued to mine.

'Cause forever, doesn't last too long forever
Doesn't last too long forever
Doesn't last too long forever these days, hey
And I try to believe that we could make it
But trying don't work, so I just have to face that forever
Doesn't last too long forever these days, hey

I snapped my eyes shut, feeling emptied. Gutted. Depleted. As I tried to collect myself, the roaring sound of the crowd startled me. My eyes flew open then ballooned to find everyone standing on their feet, gifting me with rounds of applause. He was sitting in his chair, staring down on me like a king does his subjects. I felt his displeasure, his disdain from all the way across the room and down the stairs. Immediately, the shot of confidence I'd injected had dissipated. I had been knocked back down a peg. I suddenly crashed down from my high, succumbing to the sadness I'd been feeling before I came out tonight.

"Th-thank you all." I plastered a smile on my face and walked off. I hated the fact that I had not driven so I could leave immediately. It was always easier to resist Chance when I couldn't see Chance. Being in his presence was magnetizing.

Without delaying the inevitable, I marched around the tavern, waving and smiling to well-wishers along the way, and headed to the VIP section.

Upon arrival, I ignored all the catcalls from the hustlers and players and did a b-line to Jade. I had no clue she would be here.

"Jade?" I squealed. I did not know until this very moment how much I missed her. She was sitting at the table with Chance, sandwiched between LJ and Kecia, who had clearly permitted them to sit at our table.

"Hey, girl," she said through an uncomfortable smile. I wish I could help my girl gain her confidence. "Long time no see," she said as we embraced. "Come on, braids," she complimented me while running her fingers through her hair.

"Thank you, girl. I've just been hiding out, being in seclusion. Well, that is until tonight when Kecia came and told me to come out," I said through clenched teeth. "What brings you guys here?" I eyed Chance and LJ.

"Oh," Jade said. "I was tutoring LJ and he told me about this place."

My brows furrowed in confusion. "Tutor? Nigga, you in school?" I inquired.

"Baby Girl, don't do me like that. I'm a life-long learner," LJ got up and hugged me.

"That's enough, nigga," Chance, who had been noticeably muted and scowling, interjected our hug.

LJ scoffed, "Baby Girl, I don't know what you doing to this nigga, but undo that shit before I have to blow his damn head off." He grimaced. Jade got starry eyed. *Jade and LJ? That will never work,* I thought to myself.

"I ain't hearing all that shit." Chance stood up to his full height and turned to face me. "Yo,' let me talk to you for a minute, ma."

I folded my arms across my chest. Who was he to summons me? "Do I have to?" I challenged him.

Chance's scowl increased. He didn't say a word, he

just started walking. After a beat, I knew he wasn't playing, and I had better follow. I spun around on my heals, slightly embarrassed, and followed him outside.

"The hell are you doing here, Skylar?" he asked without looking me in the eye.

"Living. Why?" I sassed him. It was dark out and the winds were chilled, causing my nipples to pebble. I crossed my arms over my chest, trying to hug myself.

"This ain't the environment for you. Since when you go to clubs and shit? Niggas be in here strapped and you ain't got no heat on you, you half naked, and singing on stage like ya fuckin' brother ain't got enemies and shit. You think this a safe place to be without your muscle? Niggas snortin' and poppin' pills and..."

"My muscle has a family to take care of," I interrupted him, causing him to finally make eye contact with me. "He ain't my muscle no more."

Chance flicked his nose with his thumb in anger. "You testin' my patience right now, ma."

My right brow flew up in frustration. "Then you shouldn't have followed me here. How'd you know I would be here anyway? You pressed Kecia for information on me? You stalking me, nigga?"

Chance scoffed and took a step closer to me, stepping into my personal space. "Ain't nobody gotta stalk yo dumb ass. You, like the rest of yo' generation, post everything on Instagram. If I saw your location, so did the ops, Skylar," he said through clenched teeth. "This is not a game, sweetheart. You can't do what everyone else does. Be smarter."

My eyes narrowed. I hadn't even realized my locations were on when I posted. He was right.

"Go home," Chance ordered.

Instead of listening, I replied, "No."

"No?"

"No. I need to enjoy myself and forget that you have embarrassed me once again. No. I'm staying to enjoy my night with my friend," I turned to walk away.

"Then I guess boffa our asses gon' be in this shit together," he spoke behind me.

I turned back around and pushed him lightly, "Leave! I don't need you to babysit me!"

Chance's scowl intensified yet again. Ignoring the people around us, he put his hands under my arm pits and lifted me into the air like I was a toddler, and he was my dad. My boot clad feet dangled in the sky as he looked at me.

"Put me down!" I kicked to no avail. I tried kicking his chest through his body, but his long, muscular arms held me too far away.

"If you stayin' we stayin'. I need to embarrass you some more, or are you gonna act right?" He asked.

I wanted to cry. I was so overwhelmed with emotions. So humiliated. So drained. So angry. So in love. "Fine," I acquiesced through clenched teeth after a beat. He put me down with a thud and I stomped over to our waitress and began to speak at a volume that only she and I could hear. "I need a brownie. The weed kind. I need something to calm my nerves."

Amber smirked, "Coming right up."

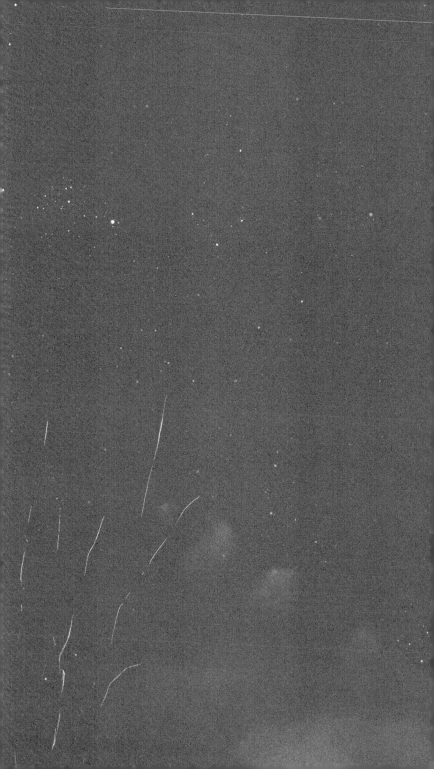

Chapter Six

CHANCE

I didn't give a shit about Skylar's attitude. I'm the one who should be having an attitude. This girl had clearly lost her mind. With everything going on in this world, she knew better than to make moves without me. I do not care how upset shorty is. Sky knows the potential threat her going around town with no muscle is. And her being around that new friend of hers wasn't security enough. History had already shown my girl didn't exactly choose the best of friends—or people, for that matter. I didn't trust the new girl around her. She wasn't proven. She hadn't even put time and loyalty into the friendship to warrant Skylar getting into a car with her alone. Who was she? Who her peoples? Where'd she come from? Was she vetted? And to go outside with this girl and post pictures with barely any clothes on in November and the location on? Seeing Skylar's outfit alone had me tender behind the ribs. Nah, I was pissed off. Seeing her church going ass on the internet in some skin-tight shit had me tight. And she knew I would be. She had blocked my phone and emails but not on social media. She knew I was still following her. She wanted to see me buckle. She wanted me to be heated. She had to. And it worked. I folded like a damned pretzel.

I'd been at my apartment sulking after going to a doctor's appointment with an expecting Nicole, hearing my baby's heartbeat for the first time. I was feeling guilty as shit having misgivings about a baby that was actually there. When I heard the heartbeat, I bowed my head and finally let the news soak into my unbelieving brain. I was about to be a dad. Of course, a paternity text would confirm this news in about six or seven months, but I'd decided to step up to the plate in the interim. I would feel worse if I chose to not be there during the process, only to find out the kid is mine down the line. Plus, Skylar already confirmed it was mine. She had that god-connection so I knew I could trust her dreams. The shit was weird. I had to tell my family that I had a baby on the way with a girl I didn't give a shit about while I grieved the loss of the relationship of my dreams. I was sitting on her favorite armchair trying to decide if I wanted to hunt down my mother to tell her the news. Would the prospect of becoming a grandmother improve her mental state? I wish my grandma was alive to meet her first great-grandchild. I knew how my OG would react. He and Jason had warned that I was going to hurt Skylar. They had a knowing deep within, and I couldn't hear it. It was like they were trying to tell me that I was incapable of loving her right—and that was wrong. It bruised my ego—deflated me. But it also fueled my desire to be everything she needed. I had something to prove to them and to me. I wasn't just a thug. I was a man, and every man needs a lady. She was the epitome of the pit bull in a skirt my heart desired.

Just as I was thinking about delivering the news to my family, my phone panged from my back pocket. It was a notification from my lady's Instagram. *Yes, I had the notifications for her posts turned on. This girl has truly turned me into a simp ass nigga,* I reflected.

I opened the app to find her in some skin-toned, fitted outfit at the lounge. Every hustler in Chicago frequented Onyx. It was the chill spot for niggas that got money and hoes who wanted to be on their radar. *How does she even know about Onyx?* I pondered. Immediately, I thought to buss up her shit. I grabbed the blick from my nightstand and stuffed it into my waistband. It was my .45 Beretta Px4 Storm pistol. I pulled my shirt over it to conceal it.

My blood was boiling, and my chest was constricting. *Who was looking at her? Who was she there with? Whose attention was she trying to garner with her chocolate ass in that chocolate ass fit?* I grabbed my phone, put on my Timbs, and headed to Onyx. I was going to drag her li'l ass out that club and take her home. Her brother would kill me if he saw her there. I wanted to ring her damn neck.

The second I got to the car, my phone was ringing. Thinking it was Lil Steve, I didn't even look at the screen before pushing the button on my Air Pods to push the call through.

"Yer!" I answered, exasperated.

"What's the word, my nigga? Where you headed?" I heard LJ's voice instead.

My face folded. "Nigga, who is you? The FBI? You following me?" How else would he have known I was on the move?

"Nah, I'm dropping Jade off at her apartment and just saw you getting in your car. I'm trying to see what the move is for tonight." LJ's overgrown ass said that shit like it was normal. Why the hell was his ass dropping anybody off on this campus?

"Who the hell is Jade?" I frowned.

"What?" LJ cracked up laughing. "Your girl's friend, nigga. The twin."

I immediately realized who he was talking about.

"Oh shit! Shorty with the lisp!" My eyes bucked. *So, she wasn't with Skylar?* That was odd. "Y'all kick it for real?" I knew he was attracted to her, but I ain't know this nigga was making trips from the southside to come on this campus and see her.

"Nigga, don't worry about it. And commit her damn name to your memory, asshole," he shot sternly.

"Is you serious right now?" I was stunned. He had an attitude over the mute girl with the dreads?

"Dead ass," he confirmed.

I lifted my hands in surrender, as if he could see me. "Look nigga, my bad. Ok? Now, put her on the phone."

"Hell naw. You don't even know her damn name," LJ stated blankly. "Do you hear me asking you to put me on the line with Baby Girl?" *Was this nigga claiming her?*

I frowned. "Nigga, and if you want your tongue, you won't!" I bucked up while turning on my car. "Put the phone on speaker or something. I need to ask her about my girl!"

I heard him pause and shuffle a bit. "Yo!" I could hear an echo in the background, letting me know the phone was on speaker.

"What up, Jade?" I greeted her.

"Heeeey," she offered a nervous singsong.

"Listen, have you spoken to Skylar? She's at this

lounge but I don't know who's up there with her," I voiced my concern.

"Honestly, I haven't really spoken to her since she and my sister got into it. It's been kind of weird between us." I could hear the brokenness between each "sh" sound her lips and teeth made.

"Oh ok," I paused and bit my lip. "Well, thanks." I didn't want to get in their friendship drama. I was barely hanging on to my own relationship with Skylar. Besides, I prided myself on not getting into women's business.

"Baby Girl be at the club? What club she at? We might as well slide that way. You wanna go, sweetheart?" LJ asked Sky's friend.

"I mean..." she went to answer.

"The hell? She don't *be* at the club. She's *at* Onyx. And I'm already on my way there." I stated, flabbergasted. My girl isn't a regular club attendee. She was just being defiant.

"Then come back and get us, nigga. You're too much of a hot head to be going up there by yourself anyway. Plus, me and Jade could go for some of them drinks up there. You heard me?" LJ reasoned.

I wanted to ring his neck for taking me off my route, but he was right. With the way my blood was boiling, I was sure to land myself in jail. What if I went in there and saw her talking to some nigga? I would beat him to a pulp. Sure, we had decided to go our separate ways, but our paths would never truly be separate. There was no way I could ever stomach seeing her being with anyone else, or having another man's kids, or moving on period. Skylar Chanel Lawson had my heart by her purse strings. And everyone seemed to know it but her.

I pulled back up to the campus to pick up LJ and the girl and head to Onyx. Those two had me fucked up when they sat in the back seat like I was some taxi driver or chauffer. They were throwing off my vibe. I turned on PnB Rock's "Selfish" and blasted it like I was on the west side. I didn't give a damn about a noise complaint. I was painting the entire Loop with my rage. I couldn't help how I felt. I was incensed, selfish, and I was unwilling to change.

Oh, oh-oh-oh, oh
Oh-oh-oh, oh-oh-oh, oh yeah
I want you all to myself
You don't need nobody else
I want you all to myself, I swear, yeah
Oh yeah, yeah, yeah, yeah
I'm selfish, I want you all to myself, I swear
You don't need nobody else, I swear
I want you all to myself, because I'm selfish, yeah
I want you all to myself, I swear
You don't need nobody else, I swear
I want you all to myself, I swear, I'm selfish

115

I want you all to myself, I swear
You don't need nobody else, I swear
I want you all to myself, because I'm selfish, yeah
I want you all to myself, I swear
You don't need nobody else
I want you all to myself

By the time the chorus came on, I heard that nigga LJ in the back talk-singing the lyrics to the song while Jade giggled and gazed out the window. *Who is this nigga right now?* I thought to myself. I don't think I had ever heard that nigga sing before. There was no way he was singing to this mute girl. I shook my head and turned the song up even more so I could feel the bass in my chest.

Now, that I gotcha here, girl
I ain't gon' play with you
Because there's a lot of things
That I wanna say to you
Girl, you know, you the shit
Balenciaga's on ya kicks (woo!)
Niggas all on your dick
But we ain't gon' trip
'Cause I'm not ready for no commitments, nah, nah
But I swear I hate seeing you with them, yeah, yeah
And I know, you ain't tryna control me

And I know, you're tired of being lonely
I can't help how I feel
I'm just keeping it real
They can't have you, girl, because
I'm selfish, I want you all to myself, I swear
You don't need nobody else, I swear
I want you all to myself, because I'm selfish, yeah
I want you all to myself, I swear
You don't need nobody else, I swear
I want you all to myself, I swear, I'm selfish
I want you all to myself, I swear
You don't need nobody else, I swear
I want you all to myself, because I'm selfish, yeah
I want you all to myself, I swear
You don't need nobody else
I want you all to myself

When we pulled up to Onyx, Fat Tony dapped me and LJ up and let us in with no problem. We never paid to get in spots like this. All over the city of Chicago, niggas showed us love. We were approached warily and with reverence because we weren't just dope boys. We were The Sinclair Brothers—Larry and Mildred Sinclair's offspring. Our name rang true in the streets—and especially in Chicago. My granddaddy built these streets brick by brick. His organization, The Supreme Disciples, had taken many boys and made them men. My grandfather had relationships with city officials and policemen. He was locked in real tight with the mayor in his day. Though he was Irish, there was always scuttlebutt about the mayor having ties with the Italian mob. Those rumors were still whispered throughout the streets of Chicago to this very day. What people didn't know was that the mayor was for the betterment of the entire city. He understood the underworld. My grandfather's organization was built to create community and wealth for young, black hungry men who couldn't otherwise find it. My grandfather had his hand on the pulse of the people. The streets answered to Larry Sinclair—and it was not a secret. Because of this, the mayor looked out for my granddaddy, and my granddaddy looked out for him. He would do voter's drives and make sure our people understood who had our best interest at heart. Everything was on the up and up until the mayor got sick, and his son was elected as the mayor of the city. His entire campaign was built on being tough on crime. Unlike his father, the junior didn't see Larry Sinclair as an asset, but like a liability. The junior made it his obligation to rid the streets of all the kingpins—including Larry Sinclair. They couldn't get him on murder, or even conspiracy to deal drugs. They had to get him on a RICO charge, which changed the course of my family's life forever.

The second I stepped foot inside the VIP section and

heard my girl singing that Jazmine Sullivan bull, my heartbeat tripled inside my chest. We sat at the table with her new "friend"—who the jury was still out on—while Skylar sang about forever not lasting when it could have. She had decided to clip our future—not me. I didn't blame her, but I blamed her ass. I saw the moment she noticed me. Her voice hiccupped only momentarily, but she sang the song with so much soul that I was stunned. I'd heard her sing, but not nearly with as much vigor and vehemence as she had tonight. I couldn't take my eyes off her. She sounded like a wounded angel— if there was ever such a thing. The intensity behind her vocals could not be missed by a single person in the room.

When she was done, I dragged her outside and questioned her. She hit me with an attitude, but I didn't care. As long as she laid her head on the campus of Davis University, she was my responsibility.

"If you stayin' we stayin'. I need to embarrass you some more, or are you gonna act right?" I asked while holding her in the air.

When she acquiesced, I put her down, when everything within me wanted to take her back to my crib and do and say whatever it is that I could to keep the peace.

"You good, bro?" LJ looked up from his conversation with Jade to ask me.

There was no way I was discussing Skylar in front of these little girls. "Gucci," I replied, but I knew my face said everything but it. I wasn't fine. I wanted to pick this girl up and walk out, but she was playing. Across the table with Kecia, Skylar was laughing and joking like shit was sweet. Jade sat next to Kecia barely saying a word.

I could do nothing but stare daggers at Skylar, who refused to look at me. She was showing out. Bad. The DJ played "Bad and Boujee" by Migos and she lost her damn mind. She stood up and started rapping like she was the fourth Migo named Pop Off.

You know, young rich niggas
You know so we never really had no old money
We got a whole lotta new money though, hah
(If Young Metro don't trust you I'm gon' shoot ya)
Raindrop, drop top (drop top)
Smokin' on cookie in the hotbox (cookie)
Fuckin' on your bitch she a thot, thot (thot)
Cookin' up dope in the crockpot (pot)
We came from nothin' to somethin' nigga (hey)
I don't trust nobody grip the trigger (nobody)
Call up the gang, and they come and get you (gang)
Cry me a river, give you a tissue (hey)
My bitch is bad and boujee (bad)
Cookin' up dope with an Uzi (blaow)
My niggas is savage, ruthless (savage)
We got 30's and 100 rounds too (grrah)
My bitch is bad and boujee (bad)

Cookin' up dope with an Uzi (dope)
My niggas is savage, ruthless (hey)
We got 30's and 100 rounds too (glah)
Offset, whoo, whoo, whoo, whoo, whoo!

She hit the "Whoo's" like her life depended on it. She was twerking her round, ample ass to the beat.

"I ain't know young Skylar was holding, bro," LJ asserted. He stuck his tongue out of his mouth while digging into his pocket for a wad of money—likely to irritate me.

"Nigga, if you put a dime on my Shorty, I will blow your head off and mail it to your mother. Family or no family, nigga," I warned through clenched teeth.

LJ fell back into his chair laughing. "Yeah, OG said you had it bad, but he might've underestimated this thing between y'all. Bad ain't even the word, bro. This is hilarious!"

"Come on, Jade!" Skylar yelled over the beat.

Immediately, LJ's laughter ceased as Jade stood up and went over to Skylar. I would've never thought she could dance, but she shocked the hell out of everyone.

Rackings on rackings, got back-ends on back-ends
I'm ridin' around in a coupe (coupe)
I take your bitch right from you (You)
Bitch I'm a dog, roof (grr)

Beat the hoe walls loose (hey)
Hop in the frog, whoo (skrt)
I tell that bitch to come comfort me (comfort me)
I swear these niggas is under me (hey)
They hate and the devil keep jumpin' me (jumpin' me)
Bankrolls on me keep me company (cash)
We did the most, yeah
Pull up in Ghosts, yeah (whoo)
My diamonds a choker (glah)
Holdin' the fire with no holster (blaow)
Rick the Ruler, diamonds cooler (cooler)
This a Rollie, not a Muller (hey)
Dabbin' on 'em like the usual (dab)
Magic with the brick, do voodoo (magic)
Courtside with a bad bitch (bitch)
Then I send the bitch through Uber (go)
I'm young and rich and plus I'm bougie (hey)
I'm not stupid so I keep the Uzi (rrah)
Rackings on rackings, got back-ends on back-ends
So my money makin' my back ache
You niggas got a low acc rate (acc)
We from the Nawf, yeah, dat way (nawf)
Fat Cookie blunt in the ashtray (cookie)
Two bitches, just national smash day (smash)
Hop in the Lamb, have a drag race (skrt)
I let them birds take a bath, bathe (brr)

Jade and Skylar held one another's hands above their heads as they did a smooth, rhythmic downward whine into a squat. They popped their knees and backs to create a butterfly effect with their legs to the rhythm of the beat.

"Aaaaaaye!" Skylar's other friend cheered them on.

LJ was relatively quiet, so I turned to look at him.

"You ain't throwing your money at the girl?" I taunted him.

He shook his head. "Hell, nah. I gotta save that shit so I can buy her a ring."

My eyes bulged as I looked at him like he had lost his mind. "You don't even know that girl."

"You don't know what the hell I know," LJ barked at me. "But someone could make that argument about you and Baby Girl, and you wouldn't even listen."

"Touché," I shrugged and continued looking at the spectacle before me until Amber came over with a plate of dessert.

"Hey, Chance!" she flirted. "Here's your food," she said to Sky.

Skylar's eyes immediately caught mine, though she had been avoiding my gaze this entire time. "Oh, you know him, huh? Figures," Skylar rolled her eyes and sat down in front of her plate.

"Joe," LJ laughed at Skylar basically accusing me of sleeping with our waitress.

"Oop," Kecia's eyes wandered around in circles, while Jade's mouth formed an 'o'.

"Yeah, Chance used to be a regular." Amber winked. "You ordering anything?"

"He don't want shit," Skylar barked and took a bite into her brownie.

"Baby Girl don't play," LJ continued laughing.

"I'm good, sweetheart," I nodded with my eyes still on my girl. She was showing out tonight.

"Okaaaaaay," Amber looked on awkwardly. "Anyone else?"

"We good," Skylar spoke up again.

"Well, if you need me, just flag me down," Amber said uncomfortably.

"You good, sis?" Jade asked, Skylar.

"Yup!" she shoveled a big helping of the brownie into her mouth.

Raindrop, drop top (drop top)
Smokin' on cookie in the hotbox (cookie)
Fuckin' on your bitch she a thot, thot (thot)
Cookin' up dope in the crockpot (pot)
We came from nothin' to somethin' nigga (hey)
I don't trust nobody grip the trigger (nobody)
Call up the gang, and they come and get you (gang)
Cry me a river, give you a tissue (hey)
My bitch is bad and boujee (bad)

Cookin' up dope with an Uzi (blaow)
My niggas is savage, ruthless (savage)
We got 30's and 100 rounds too (grrah)
My bitch is bad and boujee (bad)
Cookin' up dope with an Uzi (dope)
My niggas is savage, ruthless (hey)
We got 30's and 100 rounds too (glah)

The DJ played a few more songs while the girls did their thing. Every now and then, Sky would come back over and take a bite of the treat. Onyx was known for their fresh eats and the ambiance.

"It's... hot... as... hell!" Skylar yelled out. Her words were spaced out but very loud.

"You want some water?" Jade asked, confused. The room was pretty cool, but I knew she'd had a drink or two so that may have been the reason why she was heated.

"Heeeeell naaaaaaw," Skylar slurred. "I don't want that hoooooe to gimme shrit. SHRIT! I mean sheeeeeit!"

I frowned at Skylar. I knew she swore, but she usually did it when she was angry. Her cursing loudly and aggressively was out of character.

"What'd Amber do to you?" Kecia laughed at Sky, who was fanning herself with her hand. Her arm was moving slow as hell though.

Skylar got in her friend's face. "I knoooow a hooooe

when I see ooooone! And I know when a hoooe done been wit my maaaaan! Dass my maaaan!" She pointed at me. "It don't matteeeer what I say...dass me right deeeere!"

"Aye," I called after her. At this point I was concerned. She'd completely done a one-eighty at this table. "Let's go." I stood up and went over to her to get her up from her seat.

"Aht!" Skylar declined, trying to push me away. "Chance, I know you been giving my stuff away to that hoe! You wake her up like you used to wake me up?"

"How he wake you up, sis?" LJ instigated.

Her eyes were red, and that's when I knew, my girl was high as a kite. I looked at the brownie and realized it was an edible. "Who the hell ordered this for her?" I eyed Kecia.

"It wasn't me," she shrugged.

"Answeeeer meeeee!" Sky tried to hit me. "You been munchin' on her booooottttty like you used to do meee?"

"Nigga, you a munch?" LJ asked, shocked. "Say it ain't so!"

"I know that's right, Chance. Eat all of it," Kecia stood up, trying to give me a hi-five.

I swerved her. I wasn't embarrassed at all. I would eat a booger out of Skylar's right nostril. It was nothing to me. At the same time, I didn't need everyone in our business. She was drawing attention and I didn't need that.

"Let's go," I whispered to her. "Let me take you home, baby."

"You finna give me sooome?" She tried to whisper, but she was still loud. She was pointing down to my pants.

I shook my head. "I'm about to take you to your place."

"Uh! Pleeeease!" She was begging me for sex. "Its been a loooong time. You done gave it to your baby mama aaaaand that girl?" She was referring to Amber. "What about meeee?"

"Sky," Jade stood, embarrassed. "Let's go."

"You can't go with us," Sky waved her off. "First your sister now youuuu? Can I keep a nigga to myseeeelf? You hooooes always tryina be Skyyyy! Y'all ain't pullin what I'm pullin!"

Jade visibly looked hurt by that jab. I was tired of going back and forth with this girl. I reached inside my pocket to retrieve my wallet and peel back four-hundred big ones. I put the money on the table and picked Skylar up while she mumbled a bunch of words. I threw her over my shoulder like a sack of potatoes and started walking out. Once we were outside, I gave LJ my keys so he could drive while I sat in the back with my girl.

"Sit up here with me," LJ said to Jade.

"Is she gon' be ok?" Jade asked LJ, concerned. "She ain't never even smoked a full blunt before, let alone having an edible."

"Yeah. He got her," he promised.

I cradled Skylar in my arms like she was a baby. I was mad as hell. This was the dumbest thing I had ever seen her do.

"Chaaaance!" She began crying out of nowhere.

"Yeah, baby," I tried to keep my attitude at bay.

"My heaaaaart," she slobbered and cried on my shirt. "My heaaaart."

I wasn't sure if she was trying to tell me her heart was beating fast or if it was broken. Either way, I took the pads of my fingers and massaged her chest while I rocked her. She was garrulous, mumbling meaningless words while she cried and clung on to my shirt.

When we pulled up to The Angelous, Jade and LJ followed me as I let Sky into her apartment. It didn't dawn on me until now that I hadn't cared to find out how Kecia got home. My focus was on my lady. I took her to her bedroom and laid her down.

"Gimme kiss," she demanded. Skylar was hardly awake at this point, so I didn't even answer her. Instead, I went into her bathroom and grabbed her makeup wipes and bonnet off the sink. She would never go to bed with a face-full of makeup or without tying up her hair.

As soon as she felt the wet cloth on her face, her eyes cracked open.

"Close your eyes," I directed her. Her eyes were closed and frowned at the same time. Her face jerked with each swipe of the wipe. That's when I realized I was doing the shit too hard. I had to be gentler with her.

"My heaaaart," she cried. "Fix iiiit. God, please."

I felt like I was intruding on a personal moment between her and god. Once I got her makeup off her face, I gently removed her clothes and carried her into the shower to let the water run over her body. Hopefully, it would wake her up a little bit. Once the water came on, she clung to me because it startled her. She wet up my whole fit, but it was fine. I just had to make sure she was okay.

"Yo', you got to chill so I can make it better," I said to her. LJ and Jade were in the living room, and I didn't want LJ in here too long.

Skylar nodded her head. She was barely coherent. I let the water hit her body for a while, trying to wash her up. No one talks about how difficult it is to wash up a full-grown adult who wasn't intelligible. No cap. After a while, I just rinsed her off and gave up. I took the towel from on the door and dried her body. Bringing her back to her bedroom, I laid her on the bed and grabbed my t-shirt that was lying on her messy ass bed. I put it over her frame and laid an already sleeping Skylar in the center of the bed.

I shook my head and went into the living room to find Jade curled underneath LJ's brolic arm. She jumped up as soon as she saw me.

"Is she ok?" Jade was indubitably anxious.

I nodded. "She just gotta sleep it off," I asserted. "Can you stay with her tonight?"

She looked around the room like she was searching for words. "You're not staying?" She was confused.

I shook my head. "Nah." I flicked my nose with my right index finger. "If she was sober, she wouldn't want that. I'll check in tomorrow though."

Jade bit her bottom lip and nodded her head.

"Come on, bro," I beckoned for LJ and walked out. Leaving was the hardest decision I could make, but I knew it was the right one. Thanksgiving break was only days away. I needed to get my ass off this campus. Everything here was aggy.

Chapter Seven

CHANCE

Since Skylar's edible episode, I'd steered clear of her. The entire day was just stressful. Instead of focusing on that, I paid attention to my own reality. I hadn't been to the frat house since Zaïre and I almost came to blows. I'd become a hermit, hiding in despair. Every day was filled with more drama. If it wasn't my breakup, it was this baby. Every other second, Nicole was calling me, asking for a favor. I told her ass I wanted to be involved each step of the way. I had no idea she would take that to mean she had free reign to call me all times of the day and night. Shorty was a bug. I got calls every time she had a craving or a pain. It had only been about a month since I found out. It felt like the longest thirty days of all time. I couldn't wait to be done with her. I was finally getting a break today.

Today was officially the beginning of Thanksgiving break. I had at least five days to get away from everything and everybody. I was supposed to go to mine and my brothers' actual property, but I no longer wanted to. I just wanted to be alone in the silence. I needed space to clear my head. I had never been overwhelmed before. I was like a duck. I just let things slide right off my back. But for some reason, I couldn't shake my feelings off now. I'd been having headaches off and on for weeks. Something had to give.

Me, Jason, and LJ owned a few properties in the city, but no one knew we actually rested our heads in Palos Hills. Not even Skylar. When I came back home from New York, my brother demanded that LJ and I started investing our money into real estate. Something that was sure and legal. Lil Steve's dad had put him on game. He was making money hand over fist in the market. It was something we could do that was legit and lucrative.

We owned a twenty-two-unit apartment complex on the southside—LJ handled all the day-to-day operations for that business—our home, a laundromat, and some land out west. We were set for life.

I got up early this morning to get myself together. I never scheduled morning classes, so I wasn't used to waking up at eight. But today, I had to meet with my coach before I left campus for break. He was hounding me about seeing potential in me and I did not understand why. I knew I was smart and a good player, but I never wanted to play basketball professionally. My path was already set in stone. I was an heir to the Sinclair throne, and I wasn't giving that up for a sport.

Silently, I showered and ate a bowl of cereal at my kitchen table. As I sat there, my mind drifted to the first day Skylar made me breakfast.

> *I showered and tossed my tux and some extra clothes in my suitcase. If there was anything I'd forgotten, I would just buy it while we were down there. I decided to rock a hunter green jogging set with my Kappa Psi Omega letters on it, white socks, a camel beanie, and wheat-colored Timberlands. I was going for comfort. I hated airports and airplanes. There were too many people rushing, getting on my nerves.*
>
> *I sauntered out of the bathroom and the smell of food wafting into my nostrils hit me immediately. A nigga was grinning like a Cheshire cat. I walked up behind Skylar, who was wearing my clothes, cooking for me. I shook my head. I could get used to this. Wrapping my arm around her waist, I hugged her from behind. My right hand*

groped the same titty it had last night. I could tattoo my name on that one. It was mine now and I wasn't letting it go. She giggled in my hold, and I kissed her left temple.

"You cooking for me, girl?" I was both astonished and grateful.

"Just a breakfast sandwich. Something quick so we can go."

She slid the eggs on the buttered toast slice and put two strips of bacon over them. Then she topped it with another slice of toast. She made two sandwiches, one for each of us, and used a knife to slice them in diagonal halves. She carefully placed both plates, then turned to the stove to grab the skillet. She was really getting ready to wash the dishes after she had cooked.

"Watch out," I said to her and grabbed the skillet from her hands. I sat it in the sink and began to wash it.

"I could've done that, Broderick." She playfully poked me in the side.

"Nah. You cook; I wash. Those are the rules, ma." I said it like I knew this wouldn't be her last time cooking for me—because it wouldn't. I liked this kind of shit.

She lifted her hands in surrender. "Say less."

Skylar sat down at my small table and waited for me to finish washing and drying the skillet, bowl, and fork she'd used. Once I was done, I came and sat across from her and started to dig in. Without a word, Skylar bowed her head. I knew she was praying. She hadn't asked me to bow my head or pray with her or anything. She wasn't forcing faith on me. She was just doing her. My heart ricocheted inside my ribcage at the pure innocence and beauty of this woman.

"Are you feeling any better?" I asked in between bites.

She shrugged. "I mean yeah, physically. I still feel betrayed for obvious reasons, but I'm going to try not to let it ruin my day. We're going to Disney, a place I have never been, and I have about thirty-six hours to make it count. Anything else I have going on can be dealt with when I come back to campus."

I nodded, understanding exactly where she was coming from. "No lie," I continued to chew. "The kid is kinda excited about Disney, too." I grinned.

Skylar beamed. "Bro, it's gon' be lit. Like,

lit. It's got to be! Because who the heck gets married at Cinderella's castle?"

"Folks with money who dream big." I nodded. "You almost ready to go?" I asked already knowing the answer. Skylar was still wearing my clothes. She wasn't traveling in that.

"Oh! Let me go change right quick!" She hopped up from her seat like a rocket, then shot over to her suitcases to pull out some clothes. On her way to the bathroom, she slowed to kiss me on the cheek. "Thank you for holding me last night, Broderick. You always got what I need."

Before I could even respond to her—especially concerning the over usage of my first name—she had gone into the bathroom. I washed the remainder of the dishes and thought to myself. I didn't know what to do with Skylar.

I gulped down the remnants of milk that sat in my breakfast bowl and dropped it in the sink. I put on a black, Nike sweat suit and some Jordan One's and headed out. I was on the move. I walked down the block —because I was not about to drive three blocks from my apartment to get to Joyner—to the athletic compound. Joyner was named after the historic, Olympic champion, Florence Griffith Joyner, who people affectionately referred to as 'Flo Jo'. As I walked, my phone pinged with a text message notification from Nicole. I was hardly in the mood to deal with her ass. She'd been mad annoying lately. Instead of answering, I played music in my Air Pods and drowned out the sounds of the winds, meaningless people trying to get my attention, and empty conversations until I got to Joyner. "Damage" by Amg Manson was my song of choice.

I hung a left when I got in front of the building and went inside. I went down to the offices and asked to speak to Coach Ross.

"He's right in his office. You can go on back, Chance," the receptionist informed.

"Thank you," I offered a neck bow and headed to the man's office.

"My boy!" Coach Ross greeted me the second I entered his office. He was sitting on his desk and there was a familiar face sitting before him.

"Coach," I clapped hands with him, dapping him up. He still hadn't gotten a haircut. "How you doing?"

"I'm good. Or is it, 'I'm Gucci', like you young people say?" His rotund belly bounced to the beat of his laughter as I stood stone-faced after his joke.

"Just say you're good, bro," I stated plainly.

The other man in the room began laughing at me for being offended by Coach butchering New York slang.

"Anyway, man, this is my good friend here –I'm sure you've heard of him. Edward Stenton, this is Chance Sinclair—my next protégé if he acts right." Coach's right brow raised as he snubbed me.

Edward stood up and extended his right hand to me for a shake. "You can just call me Red, man." I took his hand in mine and shook it firmly. "I've heard many great things about you. It's nice to finally put a face to a name."

"Dope." I nodded. "It's nice to meet you too, ock."

Red was a light-skinned, tall guy with perfect teeth. His hair cut looked freshly done. The sides and back were tapered while he had sponge curls at the top. He was wearing a navy Nike track suit with navy socks and slides to match. The only accessory he donned was his signature, gold Jesus piece around his neck. He was known to wear the pendant everywhere he went. He was supposed to be this super good guy on and off the court. He wore his Christianity like a badge of honor, and many people judged him for it.

"Have a seat, son," Coach Ross said and pointed at the chair he wanted me to take.

I sat down and brought my focus to the room. "What's going on, Coach?"

"Listen, I brought you here because you're in your

senior year of undergrad. Now, I know you haven't taken the prospect of playing professionally very seriously, but I want to urge you to. The deadline for entering the draft is approaching. You need to make a decision." He took a deep breath. "Additionally, I brought Stenton here because he can tell you what it's like coming into the league in his later years. I coached Stenton throughout his four years of undergrad. He played overseas and was finally able to make it to the league. Whether you want to play or not, I think he would be a good mentor for you, if you're willing."

"Coach tells me you're apprehensive about playing professionally, which is almost unheard of. Just about every little boy in every neighborhood in the states wants to play in a professional sports league," Stenton interjected. "What makes you apprehensive about playing? I've seen you ball. You're next level for sure."

I sighed. "I don't think apprehensive is the word. I just didn't care to do it. Basketball is a good time for me. I don't think I'm destined to do it for real."

"Oh!" Red grabbed ahold to his Jesus pendant. "What do you think you think you're called to do?"

I shrugged. "I plan to take over the family business one day." I couldn't tell this nigga what my family did for a living, so I was being vague.

Red's eyes grew wide as saucers. "Nah," he shook his head. "That's not it for you, bro."

My head drew back in offense. "Nigga, you don't know me to tell me that."

"Chance—" my coach tried to interject.

"Coach Ross, can you give Chance and I a moment?" Red asked with his eyes pinned to mine.

I could feel Coach looking to me for approval, but I couldn't take my eyes off this Red nigga. If he thought he was about to son me, he had another thing coming. When I didn't look back at Coach, he got the hint and got up and left his office. He was better than me because Red wouldn't have kicked me out of my shit.

"You don't have to settle—"

"I never settle for shit," I spoke through my teeth.

Red nodded his head up and down. "If you choose to be like everyone else, you're settling. Now, don't get me wrong, you don't have to play in the league if you don't want to. But making illegal activity your life's ambition when you have another choice is settling, bro. It's weak. Niggas spend their whole lives trying to make it out the hood, and you're trying to go in? That's played out."

I squinted. "Again, you don't know—"

"I know what I see in you, Mr. Sinclair," he said with a nod, while toying with that necklace. "You're sharp as a tack, quick-witted, business-minded, and very calculated. You're trying to succeed your grandfather's rank, but that's not the life for you. God has more for you." He shook his head. "Even your grandfather wants different for you. You already have his love. You're not going to earn it being a Disciple. You're not going to earn your family's respect or love being a Disciple. You're yearning for something you won't find there. It's only in God."

I scowled. How the hell did he know who I was? Or who my grandfather was? Sure, we were known all over the city, but this nigga was a square. A church goer. He couldn't have known me. But something about the words he said piqued my interest.

I chuckled at his assessment of me. "Nigga, I don't need shit from nobody. You come in here— with your churchy ass—judging me like you know me. I'm that nigga. I don't need acceptance or love. The shit is over-rated, to be frank. I don't want to play no funky ass basketball, being owned by a league, and sold to different white, male owners like the damn slave trade. I'm my own man." I pounded my fist on my chest. "My name rings true in this city. My name makes shit happen. Meanwhile, your name is signed to contracts that only get you pennies on the dollar for what them crackers that own you make. And you want to talk to me about having my *own* path? Make that shit make sense, ock."

Red scoffed. "Pumping poison into your own people is what your family does for a living. It's a slow genocide, but you want to tell *me* that I'm bought and owned?" Red shook his head.

I had never heard it broken down like that before, but I sat there stone-faced and unbothered. My poker face was on. Never in a million years would I incriminate my family or myself by confirming any of what he just said.

"Listen," Red continued. "I'm not trying to come down on you. I'm not arrogant or just a butthole." *I doubted that very seriously.* "I'm just telling you what I see in you, man."

I shook my head. "You got all that just based on me walking in the room, huh?" I doubted him. "Nah, you're judging because I come from the other side of the tracks."

Red shook his head and sat up straight. "You don't know me, g. We actually come from the same side of the tracks. I'm from the westside. I'm from the hood, my guy. But God brought me to where I am today. God shows me things sometimes. You think I be out here mentoring niggas? No." He scoffed. "But I know God showed me you. I have a story, and so do you. You will never be head of that organization. It's going to go to your brother. Why? Because that's not you. Kingpin ain't you. You're a king. God wants to do miraculous things in your life, but you're in your own way. You won't have peace until you yield to God." He shrugged and continued to toy with the chain.

I bit my bottom lip. "Well, if god is real, He'll know where to find me, right?" I stood to leave the room.

"He's already found you. You're already starting to believe. You know He's real. He's sent you confirmation of His sovereignty." *Skylar.* "And the enemy wants to do any and everything to separate you from God and His plan. But I tell you truly, the road will be a winding one. But you're going to get to that path. The longer you resist, the more bumps will be in the road; but when you chose God and His plan, let nothing separate you from His love. Even calamity. It won't be an easy road, but it's worth every tear shed. It's perfect for you."

This nigga was talking in parables and shit. I was low key shook. Bro was OD. I had to get up out of here. "Later, man," I headed toward the door.

"Whenever you want to speak again, just hit up Coach Ross. He'll know how to find me," Red called out to me as I walked out the door.

I ambled right past Coach Ross and walked to my car. I needed to go visit my OG. I needed to talk to him and tell him about this Miss Cleo ass nigga. He was trying to cast a spell on me or some shit.

I ignored two more of Nicole's calls and jumped into my car. The drive to the prison was about an hour away. I hit the gas to try and get there before visiting hours were over. I needed to speak with my OG.

✳

ONCE THEY LET ME INTO THE ROOM, I WIDENED my stance in my Jordans, cementing my toes into the ground. I didn't know what he would look like when he rounded that corner, but I was prepared for the worst. My grandfather was sick. It was undeniable. I just prayed he didn't look much worse than he had the last time.

"Sinclair," I heard one of the guards call his name and in walked my twin. Larry Eugene Sinclair. The man, the myth, the legend. He walked in on a cane, per usual. He looked to have lost another ten or so pounds. I mentally shook my head because I could not allow him to see me down. He would clown the hell out of me. I wondered if Skylar was still praying. I needed her ass to pray that her God would intervene. I knew I had some level of audacity to be begging for a miracle, but I was. I needed it.

"Son." He lifted his chin up in the air. His signature southern drawl was still there on full display from the formative years of the life he'd spent in Tutwiler, Mississippi. He was still handsome. A light-skinned me. Tall, salt and pepper beard, well moisturized hair. It was curly at the top and faded on the back and the sides. Kind of like Red, but his curls had not been manipulated.

"OG," I threw his crooked smile back at him. We slapped five and embraced quickly before the prison guards said anything. "I've missed you man," I articulated as we took our seats.

He scoffed and waved me off. "You don't miss your old man. Couldn't have missed me. You've been moving mad funny." It's how we always greeted one another. Always.

"Never that, Pop," I smiled again.

My OG began staring at me. Just as Red had done an hour before. I needed to tighten up on my veneer. Niggas was reading me left and right.

"What's the problem?" My OG asked. "And before you say it's nothing, I already know it's something." He pulled his handkerchief out of his pocket and began hacking into it. The coughs were so violent I could feel them from where I sat. I watched his hands shake as he wiped his mouth and eyed me. *He's really sick.*

I sighed. "It's a lot of shit." I paused. "I got a baby on the way."

My grandfather eyed me with skepticism. "And Lil Steve ain't tried to kill you yet? Nigga, I'm impressed."

I chuckled and nervously yanked on my right ear. "Actually, I'm not having a child with Skylar. It's by another girl on campus named Nicole." I dropped my head, embarrassed.

His eyes narrowed into slits. "In that case, I'm surprised Skylar ain't killed you."

I scoffed. "She done ripped my heart out my chest.

So, technically she has." Sadness coated my countenance. I couldn't even hide it. And didn't care to.

"Hmph..." he offered, with the 'I told you so' gaze. "You know what you're having?"

I shook my head. "Not yet. She's four months along now. We should be finding out soon."

He nodded. "My first great-grandchild..." He began coughing again. "I wish Mildred could see this." He bit his lip. "Anyway, how's school?" My OG had switched subjects so fast I almost got whiplash.

"Uh..." I shrugged. "It's cool. I'm still set to graduate in May. I'm suspended from the Omegas because of the situation with Skylar." I rattled off the list of things that had been happening at school. "Oh, and I just met with Coach Ross and Edward "Red" Stenton, who want me to enter the NBA draft." I waved off the thought.

"Nigga, what did you tell them?"

"I told them that I wasn't playing for no league that owners can buy you and sell you like it ain't shit. I'm taking over my family's business one day." I shrugged.

"What?" His coughing rattled the room. "Have you lost your damned mind?"

"Excuse me?" I was confused.

"Ain't no excuse shit." He extended his arms. "I sent you to that school so you could have a future, not so you can relish in a fantasy."

That blow hit me in the chest like a ton of bricks. "A fantasy? OG, all I ever wanted to do was be like you—"

"STOP LOOKING UP TO ME AND LOOK OVER ME, MY NIGGA! I'M A FUCKING CAGED ANIMAL! YOU ASPIRE TO LIVE IN THIS SHIT HOLE? SOMEBODY TELLING YOU WHEN TO PISS, WHEN TO STAND, WHEN TO SHOWER? A MAN AIN'T SHIT IF THE MAN AIN'T FREE! YOU AIN'T NO FUCKING MAN IF YOU DESIRE TO BE PUT AWAY!" He stood up, towering over me. "The hell is wrong with you?"

"Sinclair!" One of the guards warned him.

"I'm a Sinclair." I pounded my chest. "An heir to your thrown. I already didn't get a chance to grow up with you. Jason and LJ had the chance to be up under your organization. I know I have what it takes to run it," I whispered so people couldn't hear us.

"Your brother, your cousin, they was built for the streets. They know how to maneuver. They *had* to be safe. You know why I let your moms take you even though she got mush for brains?"

I shook my head.

"Because I knew you was better off in New York than trying to compete for an empire I built off survival. This shit wasn't built on love."

"I ain't have love with her either! She beat my ass

149

every day! I just wanted to be with you! I was abandoned."

"You was protected!" He shot.

"I WAS NEGLECTED! You may have been in the hole in here, but I had to go in the hole in my mind to fucking make believe that you and my family had a life of bliss, that as soon as I could, I would take off and run away from my nutcase of a damn mother and be an heir to your throne!" Tears ejected from my eyes like bullets. I didn't even know I was holding them, but my OG's words triggered me. They wounded me.

"I'm trying to tell you that this kingdom ain't glamorous! Go be your own king, my nigga!" He pushed me in the chest. "Don't come back up here no more! Don't visit me a-damn-gain until you do what the fuck you're supposed to do." He stood up.

"What?" I asked, broken.

"Go, find your own way, son." He was kicking me out of a nest I had built in my own mind—one I never got to physically inhabit. I had reverted to the eight-year-old kid whose mother was having a manic episode. I was alone. Swimming in the black hole of misery, except this time, I didn't have a fantasy in mind to reach for. There was no light at the end of the tunnel. No family, no woman, no kingdom. Even the thought of my new offspring didn't give me light. I was swamped in angst and despair.

I stood there with my feet planted in the concrete jungle and watched as my grandfather limped away from me and out of my sight. I slapped the tears away from my face. How was I to find my own path when I never had a soul to direct me? Everyone was always too preoccupied to raise me. I basically had to parent my own mother with no direction of my own. Now, I was being thrust out of the cushion I thought was meant for me and told to find my way.

Getting a grip, I stomped away from the place that had been holding me for years. Once I finally got to the car, I broke again. Red and my grandfather had both called me a king, but I felt like a joker. What was a king without a kingdom. I needed to talk to somebody. To see somebody. My headache had returned to the back of my head. It was slight, but I could feel it. I tried calming myself down, trying my best not to aggravate the dull pain so it wouldn't turn into a full-blown migraine. On autopilot, I put my car in reverse and headed back to campus. I didn't want to ride in silence, so I turned on the radio. Future's "Mask Off" was the first song played on the urban radio station.

Percocets (ya), molly, Percocets (Percocets)
Percocets (ya), molly, Percocets (Percocets)
Rep the set (yee), gotta rep the set (gang, gang)

Chase a check (chase it), never chase a bitch (I don't chase no bitches)
Mask on, fuck it, mask off (mask off)
Mask on (off), fuck it, mask off (mask off)
Percocets ('cets), molly, Percocets (Percocets)
Chase a check (chase it), never chase a bitch (I don't chase no bitches)
Two cups (cup), toast up with the gang (gang, gang)
From food stamps to a whole 'nother domain, ya
Out the bottom (ye), I'm the livin' proof (super)
Ain't compromisin' (woah), half a million on the coupe (gang, gang)
Drug houses (where), lookin' like Peru (woah, woah, woah)
Graduated (crazy), I was overdue (I'm on due)
Pink molly (molly), I can barely move (barely move)
Ask about me ('bout me), I'm gon' bust a move
Rick James (James), thirty-three chains (thirty-three)
Ocean air (air), cruisin' Biscayne
Top off (ya), that's a liability (big foreigns)
Hit the gas (gas), boostin' my adrenaline (big foreigns)

I absentmindedly drove all the way to the school. Along the way, I saw a billboard from some church and scoffed. *The hell does a church need a billboard for? Money hungry asses.*

As I kept driving, I was a shell of myself— lost and confused. I had no idea what my next steps were in life.

I'd had things mapped out. The only thing I had ever wanted to do career-wise was The Supreme Disciples. That's it. There was no plan b. The next thing I wanted to do is be with Skylar. Everything else I would take as it came. I had put all my eggs in two baskets, and they had both been snatched away from me.

SiR's "This Is Why I Love You" came on and had me deep into my feelings. I had to get my girl back. I had to convince her that she could accept me and my future child. She could be happy with me—like we were before. I could keep Nicole as far away from her as the east is from the west. She just had to give us a shot. We were meant to be.

Doesn't it feel like this could be real life
If we have something to prove
Life would be normal, dinner formal
I could be happy with you
Primitive passion, human reactions
Puttin' it all on the line
This could be real life
Why do I feel like
We would be wastin' our time?
See, it's the same thing, no rules
Same rhythm, new blues
Same love but this time it really ain't love
No reason, no rhyme

No speakin' our mind
No war, that isn't what we came for

On a mission to salvage my relationship, I pulled up to the Angelous and didn't even turn the thing off. I just turned the hazards on. I was coming to get my girl out of here so we could go away together for Thanksgiving break. Just she and I. We could be thankful all over each other if she'd let me. I wanted to take her to a place where all sense and sensibility ceased to exist. To the lover's land where we could be free and bask in one another's aroma without the weight of her father's opinion or her brother's judgement—or mine, for that matter. Just us. Just love. Just becoming.

Skip the elevator, I darted for the stairs and ran to her floor. Hanging a quick right, I found her door. The lights were off, but I was sure she was in there. She had to be. The fantasy didn't work without her.

Balling up my fist, I beat on her door rapidly and with urgency. I didn't hear any shuffling of her feet, so I beat harder. She had to hear me out.

"Sky!" I shot and continued to beat down her door. "Baby, open the door!" I was met with silence. So, I kept rapping on the wood paneling until one of her neighbors came out, shaking her head.

"She's not here!" The girl yelled out to me. "She moved out early this morning. Me and some light-skinned chick helped her take her stuff downstairs. She said she was moving back home." She shrugged.

I eyed her confused. How could she have moved right under my nose. Why wouldn't she tell me? "You're talking about Skylar?", I asked, dumbfounded.

"Yeah. Everybody's going home for Thanksgiving break today, but she said she wasn't coming back," she shrugged again. "Sorry." She turned around and went back into her apartment.

I brought my balled, cold fist to my mouth and tried containing my emotions. Just as I was turning away to head back downstairs, my phone rang. Lil Steve's name danced across the screen. A bit of panic ran through me. I wasn't afraid of him, but I respected him. What if his sister told him everything? I pondered. Instead of continuing to stew, I answered the phone.

"Yerr," I said.

"Nigga, how is my sister at my parent's house and you ain't drop her off? What's she doing talking about moving back home? Who's at that school fuckin' with my lil sister?" He said, and my head immediately began to throb.

Chapter Eight

SKYLAR

Two, one
Take me back to the distance (distance, distance, distance)
Late night cooking in my kitchen
Yeah-ayy-ayy, yeah-ayy-ayy
Dirty dancing in my room
Room, room
Sending my love all over you
Because of the time we shared
Time we lost in love with one another
Days we had, pay the cost of losin'
Heart's desire, so soon
I'll be sending my love all over you

I had Yebba's "Distance" on repeat as Kecia took me home. I was so embarrassed. I was humiliated by the twists and turns my love life had made over the past several months. Mortified by the fact that I was naïve enough to think Zy would be away at school and faithful to me. We broke up in a spectacle during homecoming, which was live and in color for most of the campus to see. Then I had to follow it up by cascading into love with Chance. Only for the news of his pregnant jump off to break us up again. I decided to have a night out and due to my nervous tension, I tried an edible for the first time. I woke up not remembering much that happened the night before. The only thing I'd remembered was singing and Chance popping up on me. When I woke up the next morning with Jade standing in my face, checking on me, I nearly jumped out of my skin. She sat there and told me everything. How I acted a fool and told the entire lounge about me and Chance's sexual exploits. I was so ashamed. I just thanked God no one recorded or posted my tirade on social media. That would have wrecked me. The thought of my parents knowing anything about my behavior these past few months made me cringe.

I still get so lost in the feeling (feeling)
And I can't imagine losin' you (you)
Ooh, ooh

Oh woah, if your heart can't find a new reason
For someone special to hold onto
I wonder if I would do, ayy-yeah
Because of the time we shared
Time we lost in love with one another
Days we had, pay the cost of losin'
Heart's desire, so soon (so soon, so very soon)
I'll be sending my love all over you

After about forty minutes of Kecia's diabolical driving, she'd finally pulled up to my home. I hadn't been to this place in months. I hadn't even realized I missed it. Hadn't realized how much I missed them. My parents, my siblings, my home. Although I was the youngest and often felt forgotten, they were mine, and I knew they loved me stronger than anyone else could.

"I'll be right back. I'm going to ask my daddy to help me with my things," I said.

"Not a problem," Kecia retorted.

"And thank you so much for this. I'm going to Zelle you for the ride," I promised.

"Girl, it's fine. I just want a Thanksgiving plate if your mama can cook as good as you say she can."

"I got you," I swore and closed the door.

With the frosted, chilly winds pushing behind me, I walked up the driveway and extracted my key from my crossbody, signature monogram Coach bag. Placing it in the hole, I turned the key and twisted the door. Immediately, a rush of warmth caressed my cold cheeks. A cinnamon aroma wafted into my nose, and I immediately felt safe and secure.

"Mama? Daddy?" I called out. Immediately, I heard the sound of feet shuffling.

"Skylaaaar!" I heard my mom scream my name. I ran towards her with open arms. Why did it feel like I haven't seen my mom in three years, even though it had only been three months? She looked so cute with her pixie, cute, turquoise velour sweatsuit, and stone furry slippers. Her cheeks were so rosy and full.

"Mommy, I missed you so much," I got choked up as we continued to embrace.

"I missed you, too, baby. It's been so lonely without you." I could hear the tears in her voice.

I gulped. My mama was sad. She'd been sad for the last two years. I didn't understand it, but I knew it. She'd lost the sparkle in her eyes and was fighting to get it back. "I need to come home, Mommy," I whispered.

My mom broke our hug and looked back at me. Taking my hands in hers, she eyed me, confused. "You don't want to finish collage?"

I shook my head. "Yes. God, mama, yes. I just don't want to live on campus. I want to move back home and commute."

"Oh," her eyes darted all over the room. "Well, let's

chat with your dad," she paused. "Did anything happen?"

I shook my head. "It's not that. I just want to come home." I couldn't look her in the eye and lie. So much had happened. So much damage had been done.

My mom gave me a knowing look, which prompted me to remember her warning to me before I went off for school.

> My parents had no idea I was making my own money hand over fist every single day. My cash app goes off so much on the daily that I keep my phone on Do Not Disturb to keep them from hearing it and finding out about my side hustle. I'm in my senior year of high school. I had to stack my chips for college. I refuse to be one of those people who is doing work-study and barely has enough money for food. I knew my parents were going to take care of me, but I wanted to be like my big brother, Lil Steve, and get this paper on my own. My parents' money was for me to live with; my money was for me to play with.
>
> "Good. So, which one of y'all have a boyfriend at The Real D-U?" my mom asked and folded her arms across her chest. I glanced

into my mother's slanted eyes really quickly, trying to think of a response.

She was a beautiful, fair-skinned woman with a pixie cut, styled to perfection. My mama was the older version of what I aspire to be. She is a mother, has a husband with money, and takes care of her family. My mom is always laced in the latest designer threads. Like right now, she stood before me in a Gucci sweater and matching slides, leggings, and every hair was in place. All I had ever seen from my mother is luxury, and that's what I wanted to give to the world. I hadn't anticipated her line of questioning. My dad I had to a 't', but my mother? She was the right hook I never saw coming. Sure, I could have told her that it was me, her baby girl, who has a boyfriend, but then again, I couldn't. Firstly, I wasn't allowed to have a boyfriend yet. My parents' rule was that we don't date until we are eighteen years old and out of high school. In school, we are supposed to focus on the books and the books only. Truth be told, none of us had followed that rule except Shyanne, my oldest sister. The other reason why I couldn't tell my mother the truth is because I knew my parents would never approve of Zaïre. He was a little rough around the edges. Zaïre came from the other side of the tracks, the southside. He had more experience than me in every way, and I was headed downtown to get a lesson.

"Huh?" I asked, not able to come up with anything else.

"Skylar Chanel, I know you are not deaf. Which one of you all have a boyfriend? I know y'all are going up there to see some guy. It's Valentine's Day weekend. What do you take me for, a fool?" Her face folded. "You can tell me. I won't tell your father."

That's a lie. My spidey senses coded that last sentence before it even fully fell from my mother's lips. Had she heard my thoughts, my mother would have slapped me into the year 3021. But I knew the truth. My parents are a team. It's them against the world, including me. She would turn on me in a second to tell her teammate my business.

"Well, we're having a Galentine's Day with us girls, since we're all single. We thought it would be a good way to celebrate, no?" I asked, telling a half-truth.

"Mmm hmm..." Her lips curved into an unbelieving pout. "Well, I've been seventeen before and Lord knows I had a little guy

friend. I snuck out of the house to see him and everything."

"Really?" I asked in sincerity. "Who was you sneaking out to see, ma?"

"Steve, girl!" She giggled, referring to my dad. "Girl, I did anything just to spend a bit of time with him, but you know what?"

"What?" I asked, intrigued by her story.

"I grew to regret every moment of it. I was way too available for your dad and in his immaturity, he took advantage of the fact that I would just always be there in the cut, waiting for him. I was available every time he called, always running up behind him, skipping school to hang out with him and all. And do you know what he did?"

"What?" I was fully engrossed now.

"He got with another girl when I wasn't paying attention," she said. My mom lifted her right brow and continued, "It hurt my feelings so bad. I had groomed him just for him to tell me that I was just his friend."

"Are you serious right now?" I asked in stun.

"I would have cut daddy!" She chuckled.

"I almost did! I stopped speaking to him for well over a year behind that. I had to catch

up on my schoolwork and focus on me. My grades had slipped chasing behind him, but I pulled them all up and graduated as my classes' salutatorian." She smiled at the memory, then grabbed both of my hands. "Your dad and I didn't get back together again until my sophomore year of college. He had to beg and plead to get me back. I said all of that to say, don't allow these men to make you jump over hoops to be with them; you're the prize, Sky. Make them come to you. What a man earns, he will care for. What is thrown at him, he will play with. Do you understand?"

I chewed on the words she had given me and nodded my head in response.

"Yeah, well, I guess you don't need that bit of advice since you guys aren't dating anyone, right?" my mom stated sarcastically.

"Right!" I smiled and lied through my pearly whites.

She was right. I didn't want to hear it then, but God knows she was right.

"Well, let's talk to the Bishop," she sighed.

"Oh," I remembered. "Before we do, my friend dropped me off. My stuff is outside in her car."

My mom frowned. "Well, I can help you get it. The girls are on their way over to stay the night. I wish they would've been here to help, girl. Your stuff is heavy. I don't know why you choose to pack to the brim." My mom rolled her eyes.

She and I went outside to Kecia's car where I introduced them. My mom said few words, but she was courteous. She even invited Kecia to come over on Thanksgiving, but her family had plans, of course. It took us three trips before saying our goodbyes, but we were successfully able to transfer my belongings into the house.

"So, where is Daddy?" I asked while hanging up my Moncler puffer coat.

"In his office, of course," she rolled her eyes. "Come on."

I followed her dainty walk to the lower level so we could speak to my daddy. I could hear him on the phone the second I got down there. He was handling what seemed to be church business.

The second his eyes landed on me, he told the caller on the other line, "Hang on. Let me call you right back." My dad's eyes lit up as soon as they came in contact with me. "My baby is home." He smiled and stood to come embrace me. My daddy was a tall, dark chocolate man with a bald head and a snow-white beard. He worked out every single day, which made the muscles in his arms more pronounced in that white t-shirt. He'd paired the shirt with some jeans and brown loafers.

"Hey, Bishop!" I offered as we hugged. The hug was so full and overwhelming that we rocked side to side to the beat of our own drum. One would have thought we didn't speak on the phone every day the way me and my parents were carrying on.

"Don't 'bishop' me," he joked. "How are you? What's going on?"

"I'm ok," I shrugged. "Honestly, I want to come back home. I don't want to drop out or anything, I just don't want to live on campus."

My dad's eyes lifted and connected to my mother's. "Is there something going on that we need to know about?"

Instead of answering, I restated, "I just want to come home."

My dad nodded, understanding my unwillingness to discuss any further. "Well, you're always welcomed to come home. And you're always welcome to talk. Whenever you're ready."

I nodded my head, understanding his message. "Yes, sir."

"Well, I'll go and finish baking. The girls will be over in about an hour, and I want to be done in that kitchen before Shyanne comes in here taking over," my mom rolled her eyes.

"Eva…" my dad warned in a low tone.

My mom's eyes glanced at me then averted to him. "Bishop." She paused with her right brow lifted and headed out.

Something was going on with these two. The tension was subtle, but I could feel it. The second my mother marched out of sight, I tried to get information out of my old man. "Is everything ok with y'all, daddy?" I was legitimately concerned. My mom had been different for a couple years now, but I had never seen her "'spute my dad's words", as my grandmother would say, in front of me. Never. Her challenging him was the biggest shock of my life and I wasn't ready at all.

My dad shook his head. "I think your mother and I are going through a little rough patch because you all aren't here." He paused. "I'm working all the time, y'all aren't here anymore. With each child who moves out, things are different. Now that Selena has moved, too, there's no one here but she and I. We poured so much into you all that I don't think we know how to be *us* without you."

"We were literally married for only a few months before she got pregnant with Selena. So, we've not been in a house with just the two of us in almost thirty years."

"Wow," I whispered. *Not my parents having relationship issues*, I thought.

"Marriage has ups and downs. This is just a down we

have to fight through," he shrugged. "Your mama is lonely. I try to spend more time with her, but I have to make a living to buy all the Gucci's and the Telfars you all want."

"Yeah, daddy, but I know for a fact that if the choice was between designer bags and your attention, she would choose you," I stated plainly.

My dad looked up to the sky, then closed his eyes. "You're right." He shook his head. "Hopefully, with you moving back home, it can help cheer her up a bit, too."

I shrugged. "I can't be up under mama twenty-four-seven, but I'll do what I can."

"Good then," he sighed. "Now who is the knuckle-head boy?"

I shook my head. "I'm going to go shower and change into my pajamas."

"Mmm hmm..." My daddy said after me as I left his office.

Not only had I not seen my parents, but I'd missed my sisters as well. It was the night before Thanksgiving, so we decided to have a pajama party—just us girls—with plenty of tacos and margaritas on deck. We decided to do it at the parents' house because there was plenty of room for us to move around and be free agents. My dad had taken my mom out on a date, and we had the place to ourselves. I played the role of the DJ, playing the latest jams and teaching these old hags how to do TikTok dances. They looked a mess while trying to execute the moves, but it was all in good fun.

Ahh (pressure)
Mmh (pressure)
Ooh-ooh, ohh (pressure)
Yeah, yeah, yeah, yeah, yeah (come on)
(Y'all know what this is) (said you better)
Keep your eyes on me, eyes on me
Apply that (pressure)
Get it, don't be timid
When you in it 'ply that (pressure)
Love up on it, nibble on it, leave it (pressure)
I don't want no drip (come on), baby
Spray it like you mean it (said you better)

"Ooooh," Selena whined her hips, trying to emulate the moves I was teaching while Ari Lennox's "Pressure" played on the television.

Selena was my oldest sister. She was engaged now to her on-again-off-again boyfriend, Kyle. They were set to get married next year. Selena was a vault. She housed everyone's secrets—including her own. My sister was a listening ear to everyone in the family, and never failed to give sound advice. Her pink night gown and sock combo was super dainty and feminine.

Shyanne stood up and took the microphone we had purchased and began singing along with the sexy lyrics.

So fine and spicy, baby
Jump up on this (pressure)
I guess that's why you like it, baby
Come and get this (pressure)
Takes a lot to excite me, baby
Give it all you got (pressure)
I'm a tough cookie, baby (come on)
Hit the right spot (said you better)
Why you texting me, you know I won't reply? (Pressure)
Why you ain't fuck with me when I wasn't this fly?
(Pressure)
Now I'm on top and now I'm riding sky high (pressure)
Don't need nobody but I'll take you down tonight (come
on) (said you better)

Shyanne was the second oldest, but she was the mother hen of the sisters. Her baby blue onesie show-cased her naturally vixen-like shape. She was the first of the crew to get married. She wanted to have children, but an endometriosis diagnosis stood in her way. That discovery had changed my poor sister. She and my mom were more alike than they realized. They were both broken crayons that still colored, but they were broken, nonetheless. I admired their strength, but I simultaneously had a great deal of compassion for them.

Tajma was as big as a house, carrying triplets. She was my brother, Lil Steve's, fiancée. She was the dancer of the crew. She already knew all the dance trends. My sis had her own dance studio for kids.

"Come on, Sky," Tajma challenged me as she began to heel-toe to the beat of the song. Her chocolate skin was gifted a glow from the children she bore. With her full belly on display, her cropped, grey pajama set looked comfy and cute on her.

And I'm okay with being nasty (pressure)
Too fucking hot for all these clothes anyway (pressure)
My body dripping, boy, but you gon' have to wait
(pressure)
But when you get it, lick it like a candy cane (come on)
(said you better)
Keep your eyes on me, eyes on me
Apply that (pressure)
Get it, don't be timid
When you in it 'ply (pressure)
Love up on it, nibble on it, leave it (pressure)
Said, I don't want no drip (come on), baby
Spray it like you mean it (said you better)

We all sang the "And I'm okay with being nastay"

part of the song with glee. I knew these hoes were nasty. Especially that Shyanne. Her and Darrien are off the chain and couldn't nobody convince me otherwise.

"Let's play Never Have I Ever!" Selena shouted over the music.

"Oooh yeah! I get to be in you heifers' business," Shyanne rubbed her hands together mischievously.

"Oh, Lord," I groaned. "Let me go get the drinks." I went into the kitchen to grab the pitcher of margarita mix and a bottle of water for Tajma. "Who needs a refill?" I asked while prancing back into the family room.

"Meeee!" Selena sang while holding her cup in the air.

"I have enough," Shyanne said.

"Let me get that water," Tajma ordered.

The music was still playing, but I turned the volume down as the girls and I all got cozy on the pallets we created on the floor. Tajma stayed on the couch though for the sake of back support.

"I'll go first," I cleared my throat. "Never have I ever cheated on a test." I glanced around at all the ladies.

"Oh, girl," Shyanne waved me off as all the ladies took a sip.

Selena went next. "Never have I ever cheated in a relationship."

"Now, it's a party!" Tajma said and looked around at everyone. Only I took a sip.

"Who you cheated on?" Shyanne asked.

"Aht!" I chastised her. "That ain't how it go!"

I then noticed Tajma taking a sip of her water.

"WHO YOU CHEATED ON?" I asked in a high-pitched voice. I knew it better not have been my brother.

"Nobody," she shrugged. "But if you ask Lil Steve, he'll say I cheated on him during our breakup. Chile, he's so dramatic."

"He ain't wrong though," I rolled my eyes. "Ain't no breaks. What's mine is mine." I shrugged.

"Anyway," Tajma waved me off. "Never have I ever been cheated on," her right brow went up and met her hairline.

I took a series of huge gulps of my margarita.

"Dang, Sky!" Tajma winced at my drinking.

"Look, Skylar. Are you sure you're okay?" Selena asked.

"Whatever's said in this room won't leave this room, alright?" Shyanne added. "We're your sisters. You can talk to us."

I sighed. I pondered on whether I would share the gritty details of my life of late with them.

"Y'all can't say nothing. Never. Not to daddy, Lil Steve, your men. NOTHING! Okay?"

"I swear," Tajma looked me in my eyes and agreed.

"No judgment, no telling," Shyanne avowed.

"You *know* I ain't saying nothing," Selena retorted. And I did.

I sighed. "I guess I needed liquid courage to tell y'all," I took another sip. My lips formed a pout at the taste of the tart libation. "Y'all know I was dealing with that nigga Zaïre from my high school, right? Well, I went to Davis University because that's where he attended school, only to get on campus and find out he had a whole 'nother girlfriend."

"Dang..." Shy offered her sympathy in between sips.

"I was so hurt; but if I'm honest, my heart was transitioning away from him anyway," my eyes glossed over at Selena because she already knew.

"Transitioning?" Tajma asked.

I nodded my head.

"Yeah..." I swallowed a healthy helping of air. "I done fell in love with Chance." I palmed my face.

"Who?" Tajma asked.

"Your man's best friend's brother!" Shyanne exclaimed. She was in shock.

"Oh shit!" ejected from Tajma's mouth. We all looked at her like she had lost her mind. My parents didn't allow foul language in their home. "Oooh! My bad, y'all. I just wasn't expecting that. I just know Lil Steve's gonna kill you."

"Lil Steve better mind his business." Selena warned.

"But that's not it," I bit my bottom lip as tears began

to form in my eyes. "I lost my virginity to him after Lisa and Rashawn's wedding."

"WHAT?" all the girls exclaimed.

"And that's still not it. When it came out that me and Chance had started to date, people on campus were talking about me behind my back. I was all kinds of whores and homey hoppers behind my back, right? I was embarrassed, but I was going to be okay if I had him. You know?"

"I know the feeling, girl," Selena said.

"We know you do," Shyanne retorted.

"Y'all, I am in love and I can't shake it," I shook my head.

"Well, what do you love about him?" Shy asked.

I took a moment to ponder her question. "I love this man for many reasons. But...it's the luxury he provides by giving me the freedom not to decide things. He's always in control. And it's not in an overbearing way, but I don't have a single care, want or need even when we aren't in the same space. I can just *be*, you know?"

"I feel the same way about your brother," Tajma agreed.

"Anyway, it all came crashing down." I tucked my lips into my mouth. "It all came crashing down when I found out I was pregnant."

"Hold the phone!" Tajma exclaimed.

Both Shyanne and Selena's mouths hit the floor. I could just see the concern in their eyes, and I began to sob. I cradled my face into my hands and wept as DJ Snake's "You Are My High" played softly in the background. The girls were silent. Stunned. And I couldn't blame them.

You, you are my high
'Til the end of
You, you are my high
'Til the end of
You, you are my high
'Til the end of
You, you are my high
'Til the end of
You, you are my high
'Til the end of
You, you are my high
'Til the end of
You, you are my high
'Til the end of
You, you are my high
'Til the end of

I felt arms surrounding me. One pair. Then two. Then three. My sisters had enveloped me into a cocoon of love, and I hadn't even told them the worst part yet.

"Y'all," I cried harder. "That's not even the worst part."

"Did you?" Shyanne asked me through tearful eyes. My sister, who wanted a child she could not conceive, was asking me if I had terminated a pregnancy I did not want.

I just bowed my head and didn't say a word. I couldn't. I didn't have the strength to say the words out of my mouth.

"Oh, Skylar," Selena hugged my tighter.

"I'm so ashamed!" I sobbed into my hands.

"Don't be," Tajma offered.

"You don't know how I was raised." I shook my head. "I wasn't reared to do no stuff like this. It hurt me to do it. My stomach literally hurts thinking about it. I know God ain't pleased with me."

"But did you repent?" Selena asked.

I nodded my head. "I asked for forgiveness."

"Then you need to have faith in the forgiving power of Jesus. You believe he died on the cross for your sins, right?"

I nodded.

"Well, you must know that He did for that sin, too. He didn't die for your other sins and leave you to fend for yourself when it came to abortion," Selena stated. "You did something wrong, but God loves you enough to give you another chance."

"And honestly, you need to forgive yourself. That's your real issue. God has already forgiven you, but you haven't forgiven you," Tajma added.

I glanced up at Shy who hadn't uttered a word in a while. She had tears in her eyes, but she had no words.

"You're right," I sighed. "And that's not even the full story."

"Well, damn!" Tajma's arms flew up in the air. "I'm sorry but how much more can it be."

I chuckled at her. "Chance doesn't even know, and we aren't together anymore."

"Excuse me?" Selena asked.

"I did not tell him about the procedure." I shook my head. "And the day after I had it, I found out he had a baby on the way with a jump-off he had before me."

"Girl, your life is a dang soap opera." Selena took the remainder of her drink to the head.

"Yep! So, I got rid of mine, and she kept hers. It was too much for me to handle, so I bounced. Now, put that in your pipe and smoke it," I shrugged.

"I hate you dealt with all that alone," Tajma said, and reached out to rub my back.

"Yeah, me, too," I leaned on her shoulder.

We talked all night—except for Shyanne. We told one another our deepest fears, our secrets, and desires well into the middle of the night. We each even fell asleep holding one another on the living room floor. I loved my sisters—all of them. They were all a part of me.

THE NEXT MORNING, WE ALL WOKE UP scrambling to get ready for church. It was Thanksgiving Day. We always held one-hour service on Thanksgiving to show praise and honor to God for the blessings we were able to enjoy. Because of the festivities last night, we were rushing to get to the house of the Lord. We were late, but we got there, nonetheless.

"Amen," my daddy took the podium. "Before I preach, we have a very special musical guest here to sing to us this morning."

"Who is it?" I asked Shy. I was just trying to interact with her because I noticed she had been aloof since last night. I knew my sister. She wasn't mad at my decision. She was broken because she had not been afforded the opportunity to conceive.

"I don't even know," she whispered.

"She's a Grammy, Stellar, and Dove award winning artist. She and her husband pastor a church together down south, and she is a member of one of the most notable and influential families in gospel music history. Y'all, please show your love for CeCe Winans!" My dad announced.

The entire church stood up and shouted applause for this legendary surprise. I loved me some CeCe, though I had never seen her perform live.

"Good morning, Freedom Temple!" CeCe greeted us as she glided onto the stage. CeCe doesn't walk, she glides. She is a giant in the faith but small in stature. Her tresses, styled in spiral curls, were full and framed her heart-shaped face to a 't'. Her Barbara Bates dress was black and yellow and reached down to the floor. She looked elegant.

"Amen, I'm so excited that your Bishop brought me here today," she stated. "I'm just thankful for life. But most of all, I'm thankful for Jesus!"

The entire audience went up in applause.

"I just know that my life is better when I follow His lead." CeCe began to sing her song, "Shepherd". Tears began to fall down my face as I listened to her angelic voice.

All our eyes on You Lord
All our hope in You Lord
All our trust in You Lord
All we want is You Lord
Ooh
The Lord is our shepherd
The Lord is our helper
Oh-oh-oh Jesus lead us

And show us the way to follow You
Ooh
My life is better
And I like it better
When I am following You
Oh-oh-oh

By the time she got to the vamp of the song, my arms were ejected in worship. And without warning or preamble, once the song ended, the keyboardist began to play her biggest hit to date, "Alabaster Box."

The room grew still as she made her way to Jesus
She stumbles through the tears that made her blind
She felt such pain, some spoke in anger
Heard folks whisper, "there's no place here for her kind"
Still on she came through the shame that flushed her face
Until at last, she knelt before His feet
And though she spoke no words, everything she said was heard
As she poured her love for the Master, from her box of alabaster
So I've come to pour my praise on Him
Like oil from Mary's alabaster box
So don't be angry if I wash His feet with my tears
And I dry them with my hair, hmm
'Cause you weren't there the night He found me

You did not feel what I felt
When He wrapped His love all around me and
You don't know the cost, not of this oil
In my alabaster box

The sound her voice, the strokes of the piano, and the presence of God were the recipes for my cascading down to my knees.

"Lord, help me!" I cried. "Help me to forgive myself." I cried and sang along to the song. I was determined to get out of the black hole of despair I had been in. I wanted to stop reacting to life and start living. I felt a hand on my back, and when I looked up, I realized it was my sister, Shyanne. I stood to hug her tightly, and she accepted.

The worship was so high in the spirit that my dad didn't really want to preach, but he knew he had to. It was tradition.

After CeCe sang, my dad took the podium.

"My God," he said. "Please, turn your Bibles to 2 Corinthians 12:6-9. I'm reading from the New Living Translation. It states: 'If I wanted to boast, I would be no fool in doing so, because I would be telling the truth. But I won't do it, because I don't want anyone to give me credit beyond what they can see in my life or hear in my message, even though I have received such wonderful revelations from God. So, to keep me from becoming proud, I was given a thorn in my flesh, a messenger from Satan to torment me and keep me from becoming proud. Three different times I begged the Lord to take it away. Each time he said, 'My grace is all you need. My power works best in weakness.' So now I am glad to boast about my weaknesses, so that the power of Christ can work through me.

"The Apostle Paul is quite possibly one of the most prolific, astute voices in Christianity. He's the most quoted and misquoted thought leaders of the scriptures. People quote him more than they quote Jesus. He was an intellectual. Very cerebral. Every word he penned seemed to have been intentional. Yet in the beginning of this passage, he is telling us that he doesn't want to tell us what he's about to tell us."

"Teach, Bishop," my mom cheered.

"Paul is aware that the other disciples already look at him crazy because he didn't walk with Jesus, he wasn't one of the 12. But after 14 years, I have to now tell you about this vision. It is not surprising that God spoke to Paul through a vision, but the thing is, visions are met with skepticism by those who don't have them. These experiences are *subjective.* they are almost always limited to the person who receives the visions and revelations.

In other words, once I have a vision or a prophecy, I have no proof that I know what I know, I just know what I know. Is there anybody in this room that doesn't have proof, they just stand on what the Lord showed them. I don't know how the bills will be paid, but I see them paid. I don't know how the way will be made but I see it made. I don't know how those zeros got in my bank account, but I know what I saw. Somebody touch your chest and say, 'I know what I saw!'"

"I KNOW WHAT I SAW!" The crowd chanted.

"Come on, Daddy!" Shyanne exclaimed.

"Your gifts and visions can make you haughty. You think you're a star because you can sing. You think you're somebody because you can play, preach, pray, or pay. Anybody know people like that? But Paul testified that along with his vision came a thorn.

"He says, 'There was *given* to me.' He reckoned his great trial to be a gift. It is well put. He does not say, 'There was inflicted upon me a thorn in the flesh,' but that it was *given* to me by a messenger of Satan.

"Look at your neighbor and shout 'Neighbor,'" he instructed.

"NEIGHBOR!" The church shouted.

"Don't rebuke your gift!"

"DON'T REBUKE YOUR GIFT!"

My dad continued, "The messenger of Satan dropped off an ailment. This thorn didn't prick Paul, it beat Paul. To buffet means that this thorn in the flesh – the messenger of Satan – "punched" Paul. He felt that he was beaten black and blue by this messenger of Satan.

But no matter what the enemy sends, no matter how big the thorn, it has no dominion over you. Paul says it was given to him. Like it's a gift. And it's reminiscent of Job. Satan was looking for someone to tempt and God elected Job. He considered Job. He bet on Job. In this passage, it's clear that Satan jumped at the opportunity to beat Paul down. While you're going through your time of consideration don't forget the vision.

"I've got flesh, I've got a thorn, and I got a vision. Just don't let the thorn in your flesh cause you to lose sight of the vision. You're a believer. You must trust the one who permitted it. Trust the One who considers you. Trust the God of your vision. Be thankful for the thorn! Be thankful for the pain! Be thankful for the trial! It may have hurt you! But I promise it was necessary!"

By the end of that very spirited message, we were all up on our feet, dancing, and shouting. I got exactly what I needed.

Chapter Nine

SKYLAR

It had officially been three and a half weeks since I'd moved back home. Things with my parents were still tense, but I'd rather be with them than with anyone else. And truthfully, this was a great time for me to move back home. Christmas was next week, and I'd been helping my mom tone down her God-awful Christmas décor. We had a solid, silver and gold theme going on at the house. I couldn't wait for my family to see it. I made sure none of my siblings would be coming over until Christmas Day to preserve the surprise.

Being home had been refreshing. My problems were still what they were, but I felt like I could breathe a bit easier now. I couldn't lie and say I didn't miss my relationship with Chance. I'd cut off all communications with him. All but Cash App. The nigga was still sending me money. He didn't send much in the memo section these days. Just a quick *thinking about you* or *lunch on me.* I was trying to wash him out of my system, but I was starting to believe he was engraved in my soul. No matter how much I'd focused on other things, the thoughts of him wouldn't stop sprouting in the back of my head. One would've thought I had spent years upon years with this man the way my heart was aching for him. And quiet as it's kept, it wasn't just my heart. I now fully understand why God didn't want us to fornicate. I am sexually frustrated as hell. Just walking around squeezing my legs together, praying God takes me through the withdrawals, and listening to CeCe Winans' "Shepherd" on repeat when I'm in heat. CeCe and Jesus were about to bring me out. That's all I could do to quiet the storm brewing in my soul. I was trying to feed my spirit instead of feeding the flesh. I had to focus on the spirit in order to keep my head above water.

Today was my last day of classes before break. I only had one class, which was at noon. My dad had been letting me borrow his big body Benz to drive to school every day. I'd been thinking about purchasing my own for Christmas—on Chance. I hadn't spent a dime of the coins he had given me yet, but it would make a decent deposit on this pearl-colored Range Rover I'd been eyeing. My credit was good so I would probably only need to make a five-thousand-dollar down payment—if I had to make one—and call it a day.

Once I left my class and was heading to my dad's car, I bumped right into Jade.

"Hey, girl," I said with the biggest beam.

Jade smirked. "I'm surprised you still remember me," she quipped while adjusting the straps on her backpack.

My head jerked back. "Of course, I do. Why wouldn't I?"

She shook her head. "Never mind, Sky. Enjoy your break." She began walking away until I caught her arm.

"Wait, what's going on? We not cool?" I interrogated.

"Are we?" she retorted. "We never talk. I don't see you anymore unless it's by happenstance. I don't know if we're cool. You tell me." Her head cocked to the side.

"Well, first of all, I haven't really reached out because I didn't want to draw a wedge between you and Sage. And secondly, I'm really not used to you bossing up on me like this. What the heck, Jade?"

She scoffed. "No, you're not used to it. You're used to me being a doormat. And if you weren't so caught up in your own life and actually cared about someone else's feelings, you would know that there is already a rift between me and my sister. We don't talk. I lost my sister and my best friend the same day," her top lip curled. "When I told my sister she was wrong for how she did you, it backfired on me. And then you practically ghosted me. And for what? You're hanging out with Kecia now? That girl don't know you."

"Whoa! Hold on!" My head was spinning because I had never heard her speak so much in our lives, and she was absolutely right.

She shook her head. "No." Jade took a deep breath. "I don't care to hold on anymore. I don't want to keep waiting to see if my friend cares about me at all. Trying to see if my friend meant what she said when she was high out of her mind. I was trying to see if somewhere underneath all that diva bravado you truly felt my sister and I were jealous of you."

"Jade—" I tried to interject.

"Like, you said we couldn't pull the men you pull. You think *I* would want a man you have been intimate with?" She shook her head.

"Girl, I was under the influence. I said all that?" I was stunned.

Jade chuckled. "Not only did you say it, but I now believe you meant it. I blamed it on the brownies at first, until I realized you said the same rhetoric when you and my sister got into it. You actually think we're beneath you." Her eyes began to water, making mine react the same way.

"No, I don't think I'm—"

"It doesn't matter anymore, Sky," she shook her

head. Droplets of water fell like a faucet from her eyes. "I waited and waited to see if this was how you really felt." She shrugged. "And I think it is. And I'm okay with that."

My mouth hung open. "You're my friend. My real friend," I stated plainly. "I'm sorry that I hurt your feelings. I think you're beautiful. I think you're extremely smart—"

"Skylar, you think I'm beneath you," she said it as a fact. "But I want you to take note that only one of us is not with a Sinclair Brother, and it's not me."

My face folded at her dagger. Who was this person before me? Jade would never speak to me like this. She rarely even spoke. "If that's how you feel, that's how you feel. I tried to apologize, but you're clearly not in a space to hear it."

"I'm not," Jade retorted and took off in the opposite direction. I wouldn't burst her bubble by telling her that I could have Chance in any way and at any time I wanted to. I just let her have her moment. Having moments was new for her.

Shaking off the sting of that encounter, I sauntered over to my dad's SUV. The second I got in and made my seatbelt click, I saw a vision before me that immediately made my blood boil.

"Can this day get any worse?" I thought aloud. I was watching Nicole waddle down the street with Chance looking angry at her side. I knew they weren't together, but the sight of them in front of this building sickened me. "This must be where she lives," I continued. He stooped down and rubbed her belly. She was happy as hell to have his huge hand on her rounded core. "She needs to buy some new clothes. That shit is too little," I body shamed her big ass to myself. She had to be about five or six months now.

Chance held the door open for her as she went inside the building. He didn't go in with her though. *Good job,* I thought. Instead, he turned around and started heading in the opposite direction. Suddenly, he paused and started looking around like he was searching for something. I was so happy he couldn't see me since my dad's windows were tinted. I watched him dig into his pocket and pull out his phone. Within seconds mine pinged, startling the hell out of me. I jumped a little bit in my seat. When I retrieved it, the phone had a Cash App alert for one-thousand dollars. In the memo section it read, "I still love you."

My heart froze inside my rib cage, and tears formed in my eyes. I had never cried so much in my life. He really loved me. When I looked up from my phone, Chance was gone. Gone about his day, doing whatever wherever, but he left me with a piece of him. Just the fact that he thought about me in the middle of the day made me feel beautiful. He was the type of man that could promise you the moon and you'd believe he would bring it to you. But I guess it just wasn't meant to be. *Damn.*

CHANCE

Today was my first day of mentorship with Red and he was already messing up. The nigga told me he wanted to pick me up so we could talk. Hell nah, that's mad sus. Besides, I had to take Nicole to a doctor's appointment. She was officially five months. Today, we received the news that the pregnancy was high risk due to her developing gestational hypertension. There was a chance she would have the kid early, but I was keeping my hopes up for a safe delivery.

It had been determined that we were having a boy. I was having an heir with someone I couldn't stand, but I was having an heir, nonetheless. I was officially beginning to get excited about the arrival of my prince. I was building this kingdom from scratch. So far, there was a king and a prince. I just had to keep hope alive that I would find my queen. The idea of who I thought it would be before was now obsolete. I was starting this thing over. So, when I got the blow from my Grandfather, the next night I was so restless. Lil Steve called me and asked why Skylar had moved back home. I told him she didn't mention it to me, which was the truth.

I was tired and drained in that area of my life, so I

clearly didn't know what I was doing. I decided to take Red up on his offer. What was the worst that could happen?

I walked into Joyner and spotted Red right away. We immediately began chopping it up. I could get used to having a mentor. This nigga had food on deck for us. It was some vegan restaurant from this place called Can't Believe It's Not Meat. It was Black-owned, too.

"So, how long've you been vegan?" I asked while biting into my Big Mic.

"Hmm... About ten years," Red said as he popped a fake shrimp into his mouth.

"Dope," I acknowledged. "I could never do that though. I like steak and potatoes too much, son." I laughed.

"Man, I understand all too well. I miss chicken," he shrugged with a smile. "But it's about the discipline for me."

"Hmm..." I pondered.

"Anyway, man, let me ask you this: is there anything you're passionate about? I think that's a good place to start. Maybe that'll help you find your calling," Red took a sip of water.

I shrugged. "If I'm honest, I'm not passionate about any*thing*, I've only been passionate about someone."

"And who was that?"

"She *is* my lady, but we're not together right now."

"And why is that?"

I went through the entire story about Nicole and Skylar. I even told the nigga about Sky gifting me her virginity.

"That's sad, bro," he said. "But it may not be altogether too late for y'all."

I scoffed. "You don't know Sky. The girl is stubborn as hell."

"Is she stubborn or is she smart for not being tied to a kid whose mother hates her?" Red asked.

"Stubborn. Because she's supposed to love me regardless."

"I guarantee you the love hasn't faded it, but she's thinking with her head, not her heart," he took another sip. "Let me ask you something. If you found out she was pregnant by her ex—"

"Impossible. He never hit," I shrugged.

"But if he had, would you stay?"

I pondered over his question and yanked on my right ear. "I don't know."

"That's honest."

I shrugged. "What Imma lie for?"

"Well, what do you love about her?"

I put my burger back in the paper and leaned back in my seat. I closed my eyes and began to list the first things that came to mind. "Everything. I miss her friendship. I miss her anger. She would go off in the blink of an eye. I miss her physique. She literally fits me to the hilt. Her curves. Her brown breasts with the high nipples. Titties shaped like the teardrop tat under the corner of my OG's right eye. They were small enough that she never had to wear a bra, but she shouldn't do that. Her chocolatey nipples came out to play, refusing to hide behind even the thickest of fabric. They always went out of their way to speak to me. I miss that shit." My mouth watered, and that's when I realized I had said too much. I was going through sexual withdrawals. I opened my eyes and connected mine with his. He looked like a deer in headlights. "Nigga, don't get no ideas about my woman. I was just having a moment."

Red lifted his hands in surrender. "I don't want no smoke with your lady." He chuckled, but I wasn't playing. "But I did notice something. You didn't just take her virginity, she took yours, too."

I scoffed. "A'ight, cuz. You trippin' for real. I've been fucking since I was thirteen." I waved him off.

"Right," he said it slowly so I could get the memo. "You've just been screwing those other girls and women. What you and Skylar did was make love. She's the first person you made love with."

My mouth formed an 'o'. He was right on the money.

"Imma just be real with you, bro—I'm going to make two suggestions: the draft and abstinence."

"Abstinence?" I frowned.

"Yeah, abstinence. Any man who is a slave to his sexual urges is not a focused man. Focused men are powerful men," Red recited.

"I'm all man." I bossed up.

"Then prove it." Red shrugged. "Everything you described Skylar as was physical. How's her mind? How's her soul? What's up with her spirit?"

"She goes to church."

Red asks, "But do you? You know God? Because the best way to get to a church girl is by asking the Father. Moreover, take the focus off getting her. She's not some conquest."

"But she is my consolation prize. After all the shit I've been through, being with her is my pot at the end of the rainbow. If God is so real, He would let me have the gold after all the dark nights, ock."

"But right now, your focus needs to be you and God. I'm telling you what I know. When you get that relationship straight, everything else will find its place."

Chapter Ten

CHANCE

One month later

Thanksgiving Day just proved to be another day. In fact, the last month all seemed to blur together. Between going to the doctor's appointments with Nicole, going to class, and my meetings with Red, it felt like my life was moving in fast forward.

Today though? Today was Christmas. My family was never big on the holiday—probably because we were never really in one place at the same time. Nothing special. My brother would likely kick it with friends after his charity work. He and Lil Steve always fed the homeless on Christmas. I just sent donations. I wasn't about to stand in the cold for nobody.

LJ had Jade, which still blew my mind. I did not know what they were doing, but I just knew I saw my cousin on the campus of my college more than I did at his house.

Me? I was rolling dolo. Red had invited me to come to his mom's place for Christmas, but I respectfully declined. For one, I didn't know them folks; for two, I wanted the solitude. My life had been catastrophic lately. I was determined to watch Scarface, Menace to Society, and Boyz n the Hood, ignoring my baby mama in peace. That was the full itinerary. I didn't wake up until two in the afternoon. I was home—in my own space—in all its glory. Looking around at all the charcoal walls and decor, I felt at home. I only had black accents here and there. But gray? That was my color. It was neutral and dark. I turned the lights just like I liked them—dim. I'd even ordered Pizza Hut. The pizza ain't really good, but my childish ass was in the mood for that cheese in the crust. That shit was top tier.

Just as I grabbed the remote, I heard my front door opening. Without a second thought, I grabbed the burner from my coffee table and aimed it. If anyone was going to boldly enter my sanctuary, they must've been ready to take that trip to the coroner. No if, ands, or buts about it.

"Nigga, put that shit down," Jason said with amusement in his voice, as he stepped towards me wearing some light blue jeans, a Fendi belt, a white button up, and Fendi loafers.

"Nigga, you can't knock?" I asked with the gun still aimed at him. "And the door was locked."

Jason waved me off. "I picked the lock to see if I still got it." He took his sweet time sitting on my couch, making himself comfortable, then he dug into my pizza box and grabbed a slice of my sausage pizza. This nigga took a bite and reclined back onto the sofa like shit was cool. "Oh snap! You must be in your feelings. You watching Scarface?"

I scoffed, finally putting the gun back on the table. "I needed a little pick me up." I shrugged. "But nigga, this ain't no buffet. I ain't offer you no pizza. Didn't yo' ass just get through feeding the homeless? You ain't get no plate from them niggas, with your over-dressed ass?"

Jason eyed me quizzically and took another bite. "Nigga, I came to give you your Christmas gift. And I'm gon' eat a slice 'cause I want to."

"Christmas gift?" I looked at him like he was an idiot. "When the hell did we start giving each other gifts, money?"

"Since today," he shrugged. "I'm sick of yo' as moping around here. Let's go get your girl back."

My head drew back. "Nigga what? I told you she don't want me because of the baby."

Jason shook his head. "Nah, she still loves you. I saw

her today. She was looking just as miserable and as hopeless as you are. She even asked me how you were. She loves something about your crusty ass. Y'all need to figure this shit out or just stop whining." His face screwed up.

My wheels began to turn. "So, how is this a gift, and what do you suppose I do? She made it clear that she wasn't going to play stepmom to my child."

"And she doesn't have to," Jason shrugged. "She just needs to be your girl. If she loves you like I think she does, all this shit will figure itself out. Now, get dressed. We're going to their house for Christmas dinner. Mama Eva invited us for dinner. Skylar will never know you're coming."

I pondered over his words, then it donned on me... "Why are you so invested? I thought you didn't want me and Sky to be together."

"I don't," Jason shrugged. "It's messy as hell, and Lil Steve is gone kick your ass. However, after he does, you're still my blood. And I want to see your weird ass happy." He took a bite from the pizza's crust. "I want you to be as happy as cheese crust makes me."

I smiled and extended my hand for a shake. "I appreciate that, b!" We dapped one another up.

"You need to just tell Lil Steve though. He'll respect you a lot more if you just be honest."

"Right now, it ain't nothing to tell; but if she chooses me, if this girl looks past what I got going on and chooses me, I'll tell the world. No cap," I swore.

SKYLAR

Christmas time is here
Happiness and cheer
Fun for all that children call
Their favorite time of year
Snowflakes in the air
Carols everywhere
Olden times and ancient rhymes
Of love and dreams to share
Sleigh bells in the air
Beauty everywhere
Yuletide by the fireside
And joyful memories there
Christmas time is here
families drawing near
Oh, that we could always see
Such spirit through the year

Christmas time was indeed here. Our Naperville abode looked like a quaint, winter wonderland. Everyone was here. My parents: Steve and Eva; my sisters and their men: Shyanne and Darrian, and Selena and Kyle; and my brother and his lady: Lil Steve and Tajma. My maternal grandma, Nana Rose, was here as well. My sisters' friends, Cole and Kyra, had been here earlier when we exchanged gifts as well. Now, we had all been fed, had opened our gifts, and were just having a good time.

I was literally the only who was single at this table. The shit was depressing. I was sitting here stewing in my loneliness. I, at least, looked cute. I was rocking a burnt orange sweater dress. It was a simple pullover. It did nothing to showcase my frame; instead, my legs were on full display as the dress came to about the middle of my thighs. I felt pretty with half of my long braids lifted into a bun at the top of my head. My sister, Shyanne, had beat my face to perfection and put some twenty-five-millimeter lashes from Church Girl Summer on my lids. I felt girly and cute, with no one to look at me.

I did have some good gifts though. I got a new MacBook Pro, makeup, money, clothes, and I bought myself the car. My dad went to the dealership with me so those punks wouldn't try to screw me over. He was stunned that I had saved enough money to make a down payment. Honey, I had been saving for years. So, as we sat inside at the table, my pearl baby was outside looking crisp and brand spanking new.

Scrolling on Instagram, my brother came up behind me and put me in a headlock.

"What're you over here doing, punk?" Lil Steve said through clenched teeth.

"Let me go!" I dropped my phone and began hitting his brolic arms with closed fists.

"Say uncle!" He squeezed tighter.

I bowed my head and opened my mouth, trying my best to bite him.

"You bet not bite me!" Lil Steve yelled. He put his big hand on my forehead with his left hand while still choking me with his right arm.

"Aaaaah!" I screamed, still trying to hit him.

"Lil Steve, please leave this girl alone so she can stop screaming," Daddy said.

"Yes, please," Shyanne rolled her eyes.

Lil Steve held on for a few seconds longer until we heard the doorbell ring.

"Answer the door, Skylar!" My mom yelled, who was none the wiser to her children's horseplay from the kitchen.

I put my hands around my neck and pretended to be out of breath, while standing up to do what my mama said. "Daddy, hit Lil Steve, he choked me! You ain't see that?"

"Choked?" My dad mocked offense. "Come here, Steven."

"Ha!" I stuck my tongue out at my brother and walked out of the living room. I wondered who was at the door. It had to either be Jason or someone from the church. Being the first family of the largest Black church on the west side of Chicago meant we had plenty of visitors, plenty folks who loved us, and plenty of haters.

Beaming from my checkmate over Lil Steve, I sauntered to the front door without even looking through the peephole. Instead, I grabbed the doorknob and twisted it. My smile immediately faded when I saw Jason at the door. Don't get me wrong, I was happy as hell to see Jason, I just was not ready to see Chance standing behind him. I eyed Jason, then lifted my eyes to Chance, then back to Jason and back at Chance. Jason looked at me then back up at Chance, who was about three or four inches taller than him, and chuckled.

"Can we come in, Baby Girl?" Jason eyed me.

"I don't know..." I looked up at Chance. His eyes were the only ones that never wavered. They were glued to mine. His panty melting aura was overwhelming. I could hardly pay attention to Jason. My heart and my Good Girl started beating loudly. I had just been complaining about not having anyone here with me—about no one seeing me—but here this man was, seeing through me and straight into my soul.

"Who's at the door, Sky?" I heard my dad yell, then I heard footsteps.

"Oh, Jason and Chance. What's up, fam?" I heard

Lil Steve say from behind me. "Sky watch out," he pushed me out of the way to bring them inside.

"It's all love, bro," Jason said, while stepping in and taking off his gray trench coat.

I basically tuned him out and watched Chance free his body of his black, puffer coat. His cologne immediately wafted into my nostrils. The nigga had purposely put on my favorite, Baccarat Rouge 540. He looked so good in his simple, white Gucci sweater, Gucci jeans, wheat-colored Timberlands, and a gold chain with an Africa pendent on it. His waves were making me seasick. His chocolate skin looked like the smoothest Godiva. Then this nigga had the nerve to lick his lips and bow his neck at me. To like, speak.

Chance and I had not seen each other since I had accused him of sleeping with a young waitress. He looked good, though he had bags under his eyes. If things were different, I would have run away with him and forgotten about everyone else. But they weren't.

I didn't return the neck bow; I just lifted my right brow. "You gotta take your shoes off." I said with plenty attitude.

Without putting up a fight—like he normally would, he simply said, "Yes, ma'am." He dipped his body low and did what he was asked. I was surprised by that fact. He was always so defiant. But today he was...different.

We joined everyone else in the dining room. When Chance's tall stature stepped into the room, all of my sisters' eyes immediately found mine in questioning stares.

"I THINK WE'RE GOING TO GET OUT OF YOUR hair, Bishop and Lady Lawson. Thank you for having us," Jason said.

"Yes, ma'am. Everything was delicious," Chance concurred.

Who was this man before me? When had this criminal started calling folks ma'am and sir? On the other hand, I could not have been happier that Chance and his brother were getting ready to leave our dinner table. I was conflicted as hell. This was the first time my head, my heart, and my Good Girl weren't on one accord, and I didn't know which one of these heifers to listen to. My heart just wanted to get up from my seat, saunter over to him, and crawl into his lap. I just wanted to wrap my arms and legs around his person and let him cradle me while I listened to the sound of his heartbeat. My nipples pebbled at the thought of being in his personal space. And it didn't even have to be sexual contact—just contact. On the contrary, my head wanted to run. My armpits had been misting this entire evening with nervous energy. I felt him staring at me, beckoning my attention. But I could do nothing more than offer a few glances at a time. I noticed him. I saw him. He'd grown out his beard in the last couple of months. Damn did he look good. His white teeth shone through the room. Every time I caught him licking his lips, I wanted them on me. Everywhere. It was all bad. I was all gone. As much meditation as I had been doing, a CeCe Winans song hadn't come to mind all evening. It was Color Me Badd's "I Wanna Sex You Up", Evelyn Champagne King's "Love Come Down", and Muni Long's "Hrs. and Hrs." I never stopped being attracted to Chance; it was his circumstances that gave me pause.

"Jason, let me holla at you, bro," Lil Steve said while raising up from the table with them.

"Thanks for the invite, ock," Chance's heavy voice broke through the chatter while he dapped my brother up.

Tajma nudged me in the side, urging me to speak to him, but I couldn't. "Go walk him out," she whispered.

Everyone exchanged goodbyes with the guys as they got ready to head out.

"Thank you for hosting us at your beautiful home, Mrs. Lawson," Chance put on his gentleman mask to kiss my mother on the cheek.

"Oh, of course, Chance. You're welcome to eat at mine and Bishop's table any time," My mom graciously rubbed his arm. I was insanely jealous of her fingertips, but my stubbornness kept me cemented to my seat.

"You know, Jason is like family to us. You are, too," my dad chimed in.

Selena chuckled underneath her breath.

"He sure is," Tajma murmured while Shyanne's eyes bucked.

"Shut your pregnant ass up," I turned and whispered to my sister-in-law.

"Is it ok if I use your restroom?" Chance asked, with his eyes plastered on my profile.

"Sure. Go ahead and use the one upstairs. When you get up there, make a right. It's next to Skylar's room." My mom patted him on the arm and ushered him up the staircase.

Shyanne and Selena were giving me the eye as Chance drifted out of the room right behind Lil Steve and Jason.

"What?" I whispered, while keeping an eye out for my parents' ears.

"Girl, I'm staying out of it," Shyanne said.

Tajma rolled her eyes while Selena bucked hers.

"Everything alright?" my dad asked, noticing the shift in energy.

I just nodded my head, trying to get the heat off me.

I was cranky, horny, hurting, and happy all at once.

"You sure, Sky?" My mom asked. "You're sweating. You feel okay?"

I shook my head and palmed my glass of wine. Pulling the goblet to my face, I scarfed down the berry-flavored, fermented drink in three gulps. I sighed audibly once I drained the glass. "On second thought, I need to go to bed. My head hurts." I placed the glass back on the table and rubbed my temples. "I'm sorry, Mommy. Dinner was lovely. I just need a pain pill and my bed."

My mom rushed over to me and kissed me on the forehead.

"What'd I miss?" Lil Steve said as he entered the room, resuming his seat next to his fiancé.

"Oh nothing. Just Skylar and her headache," Selena winked at me.

"Dang, Baby Girl." Lil Steve said, concerned. "You need to get checked out for them headaches."

"Mmm hmm..." my dad agreed while gnawing on a turkey leg.

I stood from my seat, breaking my mother's hold. "Goodnight, everyone." I waved at my family and headed upstairs to my room. I just wanted to sleep my feelings away. That had to be the solution to all my problems.

As I climbed the stairs, I secretly hoped I would catch a glimpse of Chance, but the bathroom door was wide open and the lights were off. I cursed myself under my breath and proceeded to my room.

I went inside with my phone in hand. I toed out of my slippers and turned around to flick on the light. When I turned back around towards my bed, the stun at the sight before me knocked the wind out of me. I dropped my phone. Was I afraid? No. But I was startled —and immediately, his presence made my middle weep. She sprinkled like a fire hydrant in the middle of the hood on the sixteenth of July. I was stupid. Certifiable. I had to be because if I were sane, I would've screamed. I would have alerted my daddy and my brother that an intruder was in our midst; but I knew, like he knew, he was no intruder at all. Chance belonged where I belonged. Playing the cat and mouse game had become exhausting, literally leaving me ill and void of life. Now, here he was sitting on my bed. There was nowhere for me to run. No room for me to hide my emotions. It was just he and I – eye to eye. And he was offering me HANGRY eyes. He was mad and he wanted me. I was upset and I desired him. We were emotional mirrors, projecting one another's pain on the big screen for us to see and resolve. I didn't want to look, but his orbs drew me in like magnets. Besides, I couldn't ignore the heat that rose from my treasure box.

Chance got up from the bed and sauntered over to me slowly and arrogantly. That shit turned me on. The tent in his pants had my name on it. I tried to play coy. I looked up from his third leg and made eye contact with him. That's when he did it. He chuckled. It was a knowing smirk. *Ole arrogant ass nigga.* He walked right up on me and stood so close that my nipples reached out and shook hands with his skin. And all we did was breathe each other's air and stare. It was so intimate. So us. This was my best friend. My heart's song. And I was about to become a reacquainted lover.

"You keep trying to act unaffected, but I smell you. When you walked past me at the table, your aroma teased my nostrils. I know that Good Girl miss me. You ain't got to front." He licked his lips and smiled.

"We don't miss you, nigga," I lied, trying to match his cocky energy.

"You don't?" He stepped even closer. His stomach smashed my breasts in between us, causing my breathing to hitch.

I shook my head, averting my gaze to the lamp across my room. I didn't want to want him, but I got the "can't help its."

Without preamble or warning, Chance palmed a fist full of my hair to control my gaze. My eyes misted at the thought of what was to come. Mouth slightly ajar, I thought he was about to kiss my lips. I was eager to taste him. Shit, I'd had dreams about it; but he didn't. Instead, he whispered, "Stop fuckin' playin' wit me."

That New York accent shot through my soul. I whimpered. And what the hell was that? When had I started whimpering like a lovesick, horny teen. But that's what I had been reduced to – a whimpering puddle of anticipation and unmitigated lust. My mind drew a blank as he stood there waiting for my answer. Like, he literally wanted me to answer! This was torture. I could hardly remember my name in this moment. Why was I mad at this nigga again? Shit, anything he had done was easily forgivable with his cologne breaking and entering my nostrils, taking up residence in my heart cavity. I nodded my head, vowing to be done with the games.

"What'd you say?" His thumb swiped my bottom lip, reminding me to use my words.

"I'm done playing, Zaddy," I moaned. When had I started calling this man that? Probably when I felt his strong man bobbing against my constricting abs. It stood, sandwiched between us, ready for go time. I wanted to see my old friend. I remembered him vividly, looking as smooth and as tasty as licorice.

Chance gave a knowing smirk, then ducked his head and proceeded to give an oral assassination to my neck. I was trying to remember to shut the hell up. There was but some wood and drywall standing in between my family's dinner party and this freak session. His assault on my neck was sending shockwaves down to my toes. Then he did it. He bit down on the skin of my neck.

Then he kissed the spot. He came up to my jawline and bit down in two, fresh places. I gasped in his hold. The pain stung so good I wanted to pay his rent. Chance wedged his right knee in between my legs while pinning me to the door to keep my limp, submissive body from collapsing to the floor. My right hand cupped his head to hold him in place, while my left rubbed up and down his back. His clothes were in my way, but I couldn't even think of how to use my words to tell him to take that shit off.

Suddenly, Chance grabbed both my hands and pinned them over my head. That solicited another groan from my belly. "I don't need your help," he shot in an authoritative voice. He frowned in disapproval and looked into my eyes to cement his point. "No hands yet. Aight?" I nodded.

With his left hand, he kept my hands pinned over my head. With the right, he pulled my left leg up to his waist and ducked his head down lower. He latched on to my left breast - his titty - and I nursed him like he was my child. He feasted through the fabric of my dress but somehow I felt bare before him. Meanwhile, the festive music and loud laughter in the background didn't even distract me. I was too focused on Chance's tongue flicks and tricks. He began to grind into me.

Wait, was I really dry-humping in my daddy's house, and without making him beg for it? I am so weak! The

'D' weakened me! I couldn't even hold out for twenty minutes. He has a baby – a whole human he's responsible for. How is this going to work? I grew rigid.

"Get that shit out your head. You already punished me enough. You're my heart. We're supposed to be together. Aight?" This nefarious lover of mine read my mind like hooked on phonics.

Obediently, I nodded, agreeing to everything he said. Slowly, he backed away, and my body immediately missed him. I eyed him, confused, as he just stared at me.

Chance closed his eyes and bit down on his bottom lip, while his right hand cupped his beard. Opening his lids, our orbs connected. "Can I have you tonight?" He asked.

"Absolutely," flew out of my mouth before he could even finish his question. "Immediately, yes."

Chance gave me a sexy smirk, then said, "The best gift of all time." He pounded his fist into his chest three times before he grabbed the bottom of his sweater, raising it over his head along with his undershirt. The muscles in his arms had become a little more defined since the last time I'd seen him. The best part of this visual was his gold chain laying up against his charcoal skin. He just looked like an African god to me, and I wanted to bow down before him.

Before I could, he gently grabbed me by the fingertips, pulling me closer to him. He carefully but hurriedly pulled my dress over my head. He eyed my body while I stood there bare, wearing only a white thong. Before he could even ask, I shimmied out of them. I sauntered towards the bed and had a seat. I was tired of waiting. We'd waited too long. He didn't follow me though. He just stood there gazing.

"Did you change your mind?" I whispered.

Chance didn't reply. Instead, he went over to my bedroom door and locked it. *At least one of us is thinking,* I reasoned to myself.

Finally, Chance removed his belt with anal precision. Then his jeans and underwear came down in one swoosh. He folded them up and put them on my armchair while I grew more antsy by the second. He kept the Nike socks on—just like a nigga. He was a beautiful, beautiful man in all his glory – just chocolate on chocolate with a gold, Africa chain and socks on his feet. He walked over to the bed with authority, looking like he was carrying some serious weight—because he was. I bit my lip and squeezed my thighs together in anticipation. Chance picked up my right leg and dragged me in the center of the bed. I adjusted my head on the pillows beneath me. Chance stood on his knees in my bed and looked me dead in my eyes.

"I love your difficult ass," he frowned and palmed my face, leaving his thumb in between my teeth.

"I love you, too. Still," I said, though it sounded

muffled. Chance leaned down and finally took my mouth. Our kiss was so raw, so vulnerable. Both of us using our tongues to climb ourselves back into one another's lives. Licking away complications and washing away fears.

Without my permission, Chance's hands reached up and fingered my bun. A heap of braids swam down to find their place on my head. Chance moved the ones that were in my face and tucked them behind my ears. "I like you like this."

The room began to spin when he sucked my lip away from my face, then bent down to bite my chin. I gasped when he licked the pain away.

"Knees up," he instructed, and I obeyed. I pulled my knees up to my chest and wrapped my arms around my thighs for good measure. This was my favorite part.

Chance got down in the prone position, looked me in my eye, then kissed my pearl. "You been starving a nigga," he said angrily.

He wasn't playing fair at all. Doling out sweet lashes, solidifying our relationship with each one.

"I'm sorryyyyyy," I whimpered while he tongued my fountain as my family partied downstairs. He took his time on me. Like service, he was devoted, and focused. Chance worshipped my wet like I worship my God - in spirit and in truth.

"Ooooh.." I went along for the ride as he flew me to

Jupiter and Mars. I gave up the duty of holding my trembling legs. Instead, I let them rest on his round, toned shoulders.

I closed my eyes, relishing in the feeling of us being together. Finally. Becoming us again. Finally. I opened my eyelids and batted them, trying to make sure I hadn't been dreaming. I had to verify the validity of this juncture. We'd been fighting for so long that fighting felt normal. Anger felt customary. Our circumstances had pushed us into opposite sides of the ring, causing us to war against one another. I never hated him. He couldn't possibly hate me. We were so passionate about each other, had so much fire burning in our hearts for one another, that when everything around us didn't work in our favor, it caused us to burn one another in our efforts to get away. My heart didn't know the difference. Whether my head was in the corner or in the center of the ring, my heart was still beating in the palm of his hand. His movements massaged it, causing it to continue to beat even if the beating was murmured.

My eyelids fluttered open and my eyeballs hit the ceiling. The sting of my emotions caused my orbs to sting with tears. I took a deep breath to distract myself from the tender feelings that were trying to warm me when I felt a pull from my nether regions that lured my attention to the act at hand. The nigga was working overtime to snatch my soul through my body—and he was succeeding.

The second my eyes hit his head, he moved his pupils up to meet mine. He didn't even stop snacking to do it. He just winked at me. This arrogant ass, trespassing ass nigga. He was doing just what he'd contemplated as I flexed my toes to the rhythm of his gnawing.

"Sky?" I heard after three, consecutively swift raps on my wood door. My eyes bulged to triple their resting size and my thighs involuntarily circled around Chance's neck with a vengeance. Immediately, my entire body tightened in angst and anxiety. My fists were balled tightly, abs constricting, and eyes searching the room for answers or a hiding place. The sound of my mother's voice sent the fear of God—that I had placed to the side to enjoy this moment—back in me. I tried to steal my breathing, as if she could hear the sounds of my love-stricken breath on the other side of the door. Chance tried to get up, but the hold my legs had around his neck only got tighter. My panicked countenance found his amused one. He tapped me on my left thigh, trying to get me to ease up, but I couldn't. Instead, I warned him with my eyes not to move a muscle. If my mom caught me with a man in my bed, it was sure to be my last day on earth. That I knew for a fact. I would hate to finally get things right with Chance only for me not to be able to spend a lifetime with him.

"Sky!" My mom called out for the second time.

I looked at Chance for advice. "Say something," he mouthed.

I nodded my head, following his lead. "Hmm?" I called out with my groggy voice.

"You feeling any better, baby?"

I was confused for a split second. I had almost forgotten that I forged a headache to come upstairs and sleep just moments before.

"A little," I bit my lip. She didn't need to know I was feeling like heaven's trespasser, getting all the pleasure in the world in the wrong way. "I was 'sleep," I lied through my teeth in an effort to end the conversation. Chance had begun rubbing my booty, which forced me to loosen my grip around his throat.

"Ok, I was just concerned. I have some Ibupro—" I started to drown my mother out as Chance reacquainted himself with my Good Girl. He was sitting back on his legs, making a ninety-degree angle while he held my behind in his big, black hands. He was taking helpings of me like I was the last slice of my grandma's chocolate cake. Greedily, he held his dish to his face while my head remained on the pillow. We looked like a triangle of love and lust. Feeling the temperature of my body overheating, I touched his carpeted hair, hoping he would get the hint to stop, but he only shook his head out of my hold. I was so caught up in the rapture of his love that I couldn't move. I twisted and turned until I became like a volcano in his hold. I became undone all over him. I was spent as he let my body fall to the bed; but he wasn't finished with me yet.

As I focused on catching my breath, Chance rushed up offering me his filthy mouth, feeding me my own nectar, while entering my Eden. My eyes bucked open. It took everything in me to stay quiet. I would die if we were caught for real this time.

"Chance..." I whispered his name as he pressed his forehead into mine.

"I don't want to be without you no more," his lips grazed mine with each word. "I miss us." He kissed me.

Tears fell from my eyes as we united in oneness. I couldn't run from him if I wanted to. I belonged here. I belonged in this union. With each movement, as he loved me to life, he gazed down into my eyes. I didn't even mind the fact that his gold chain strummed my eyelashes with the same rhythm that he strummed our somatic song. I loved it. I was the only person that got to experience his gangster and his gentleman. The nigga was an African god. A warrior. At this point, I could look past a baby. I could look past a multitude of his sins. Hoes could call me every type of stupid known to man; they didn't know this love. They didn't know this pain. They couldn't feed my soul like he could. I'd give a toe if it meant my heart could feel this full. I'd been on empty without him; but here on Christmas, he was here to fill me up.

"I need us," I cried. It was more like a weep. I was so vulnerable, so open, so free. I could never do this with anyone else. I could never have a little snot escape my nose while being intimate with anyone else. With *thee* one, it didn't even matter. He thought the ugliest parts of me were the best ones. "Chance, I need us, babe." The man was serving pleasure and pain in equal serving sizes.

"Who?" He frowned. He bit my cheek and spun me around. I almost crawled away until he fisted my hair, pulling my face to his. The sheen of our perspiration made me stick to him like glue. "Who?" he asked again with his face plastered next to mine.

"Chance," I whispered. I lived to aggravate this man.

Chance chuckled, knowing my game all too well. "Imma ask you one more time," his teeth bit down into his bottom lip with authority. "And you better get it right this time." His left hand left my hair and went around my neck as he bit down on my ear. "Who am I to you, Sky?"

"Okaaaaay, Broderick," I groaned. "Rude ass."

He kissed me as we ascended into the high heavens. If God created something better than this, He left it up there with the angels.

"I'm in love with you." He said as his back stiffened. "Got me acting up in yo' daddy's house."

"You deserved it though, king," I planted a kiss on his arm. In that moment, I couldn't even focus on making sure we weren't caught. I just had to bask in the essence of the meeting of our bodies, consequences be damned.

Chapter Eleven

CHANCE

Skylar had been asleep for about three hours now. The sounds of the music from the festivities had ended about an hour ago. I could not believe I was laying in her bed in her parents' crib with her lightly snoring in my arms. It was a sound so beautiful and so freeing. I wish I could stay like this all day. It was four o'clock in the morning. I knew I had to get out of here so her folks wouldn't catch me up here with her.

What Skylar was holding was more that just a pussycat. Her feline had tamed and trained my hoe ass. I didn't look at sex the same way I had before her. It used to be something to do, but it was now an experience, a connection, a frequency. Though she was virtually inexperienced before, somehow she carried all the proponents it takes to satisfy me. I get off on her get off. She's the first person to get me out of my selfishness and go through lengths to pleasure her. Her folds envelope me into a cocoon of love I never want to break free from. And I know she's destined to be my wife because we fit. Nah, the Good Girl ain't just a lil pussycat, she's a fucking lioness.

I was so tired. I wanted to join her in her peaceful slumber, but fear of getting found out kept me awake. Her mother coming up here in the middle of me feasting on her was wild enough.

Last night, we went for three rounds of bliss, solidifying and cementing our love into the winds. Skylar's name had been engraved on my heart, and it was never leaving. I couldn't believe this shit was real or true. I couldn't believe I was here with her or that she had chosen me. I lifted her right hand and kissed her knuckles. Just to see if she was real. To see if I was dreaming. I couldn't believe that she was finally mine and I was lying next to her and had made love to her. The squirm that she did was the pinch to let me know this was real life. Her ample jatty scooted back into my lap as we spooned. That woke him right up. I grew rigid in the fold of her firm behind. Something about Skylar made me more lecherous than I'd ever been. Every time I saw her, I wanted her.

I wished I could be as loud and as boisterous with

our lovemaking as I wanted to be...how we used to be, but quiet would have to do. Red said a man who was controlled by his sexual urges wasn't a focused man. However, I wasn't controlled by lust; I was controlled by *this* woman. Her moods dictated my day. Her impulses strongly influenced my decisions. If that made me a slave then I didn't give a shit. Red could kiss my ass.

I slithered my body down to the end of the bed like a serpent. I was eager to wake her up for old time's sake the old-time way so I could get back to my place. I wish I had some music playing, but the sounds of her love coming down would be enough to serenade us.

On my knees at the end of the bed, I gently turned Sleeping Beauty on her back and began to feast. I moved my tongue like a snake, invading her garden of Eden. It only took three *hiss*es before she stirred awake.

"Chance..." her eyes fluttered open. "What are you doing?" She knew exactly what I was doing because her right hand reached down and rubbed her fingers through my waves. Fucking it up. I didn't care though. She could do whatever she liked.

"You," I replied, making her womanhood pop.

Sky moaned. She knew what it was. She was my buffet. This was the only thing that made me think her god was real. The way she reacted to me was nothing short of divine. How I imagined it was up there beyond the skies. Bliss. Euphoria. Utopia.

I nursed on her passion, enjoying notes of Skylar on my pallet. She was a delicacy. Within minutes, she gave me her heavenly reward. I smiled to myself, satisfied with my handiwork.

"You are so nasty, boy," she stated with her hoarse, morning voice. My baby was sounding like every bit of Whoopi Goldberg this morning. Like she'd had twenty cigarettes the night before. But that was fine with me. I loved her past it.

I chuckled while getting up from the bed and grabbing my clothes. I went over to the chair where I left them folded and put on yesterday's look. I hated the fact that her bathroom wasn't adjoined to her bedroom. I wouldn't risk it all by leaving out into the hall and showering, *then* leaving. Instead, I had to marinate in our love until I was able to get home and shower—and I was fine with that.

"Come and walk me to the door, baby," I demanded while rubbing on her thigh.

Without question, Skylar hopped up and put on a robe.

"I'll go out first to make sure no one's still up," Skylar whispered and peeped out the door. She walked out for about forty-five seconds, then came back and beckoned me to follow her out. Once we got to her front door, I put on my coat and Timbs.

"You didn't even get to shower or brush your teeth,"

she whispered, while I held her by her waist with both hands.

"It's ok, baby," I kissed her forehead. "You can live on my tongue for a little bit while I go home."

We chuckled.

"Boy, you are ignorant." Skylar rolled her eyes. "I love you though."

"I love you more," I said honestly. "Listen, we together now. I'm going to send you an address via text. Unblock me and pull up today. I don't want to spend no more nights apart, ma. And no more playing," I shrugged. "After break, I need you back on campus and staying with me."

Skylar's eyes went wild. "I don't know if I—"

I bent down and shoved my tongue in her mouth. We kissed with wild abandon at her parents' front door.

"I know you lying!" her sister Selena gasped. Skylar was immediately startled and gasped in my hold. "Sky, he stayed the night?"

"Imma go," I said, ignoring her sister. She don't scare me.

"Yeah, you do that," Selena shot.

"See you later, babe," I pecked her lips.

"See you."

And with that, I walked to the corner and placed an order for an Uber. Happy, full, and content, I was now ready to go home.

❄

SKYLAR

"Look, Selena," I turned around to face my sister. "Please, I'm begging you not to say anything."

Selena's eyes narrowed. "You never have been good at sneaking anything," she said in a hushed tone. "First of all, Daddy will be waking up in an hour for prayer and your dumb behind doesn't think he's going to look at the security footage?"

My eyes swelled. I was so caught up in making up that I hadn't considered the cameras. There were cameras all around our home to ensure our safety. I'd been so used to them that I didn't even think about them anymore.

"Oh my God! Is there any way I can get to the footage, Lena? There's no way mommy and daddy can find out. I just got an ounce of happiness back. Please, don't make me lose my life."

Annoyed, Selena thumbed her nose at me. "I'll go to the office to delete it." She rolled her eyes. "You have to stop being so careless, Skylar. Enough is enough now. Like, we all had compassion for the stuff you've gone through, but most of it was self-inflicted. I'd bet any amount of money that y'all didn't use a condom, did you? And was the headache even real or did you just say that to sneak him in your room?"

That quickly, common sense had been zapped back into me. There was something about love that makes me go absent-minded. I just want the feeling. I press play, void of all things logical, to get to what feels good.

"To be honest, I made up the headache because I didn't want to be at the table anymore, but I definitely was not expecting Chance to be in my bedroom. I literally turned the light on, and one thing led to another and... You're right," I shook my head.

"So, you get pregnant and have an abortion then you have unprotected sex yet again?" Selena eyed me quizzically. "Who is flying the kite in that brain of yours?"

I pursed my lips together because she was right, and I was ashamed. But I also did not have time for this lecture. I had to go and meet up with Broderick. "Can we get to the security footage, please?"

Selena rolled her eyes yet again and trekked towards my dad's office. "You're impossible."

I knew my sister loved me, though I was getting on her nerves. And she was right.

After showering and having breakfast, I hopped in my new whip and headed all the way to Palos Hills. I wondered why we had to meet all the way in the boondocks. I was slightly uncomfortable, but I knew I could trust him. I turned my locations on and sent the pin to Chance and Selena while I jammed all the way.

Hey boy
Let's go get ourselves into some trouble
Catch the train and take it to my borough
I'll take you up to Jupiter and Pluto
Away we go (We go) (Ooh, wee)
No one understands the way you know me
I thank God for you, you're such a blessing Now, why you
steady talkin?
Come undress me
Boy you so sexy, baby
And I love the way you just take your time
And then you read my mind
And give me what you know
I need, oh, baby (oh, baby)
I'm feelin you and I'm in love with you
I wanna give it to you
If I told you, would you believe?
Oh Oh, you know that I'm all (All yours)
I'm already yours (All yours)
Oh, Baby boy I'm all (All yours)
I'm all yours, oh (I'm all yours)

I ROCKED OUT TO VIOLET TYSON'S "ALL YOURS" as I traveled along the way. I was singing loud as hell and did not care. My face was fresh, and I had my window cracked. The city's winds blew harshly into my face. I was sure I would end up with a cold, but I didn't care. I was in a mood. I needed the world to hear me singing about my man, and I needed to feel the winds in my hair. The wind served as my fan. My tresses blew as I sang. I was on my Beyoncé – I am Sasha Fierce mode. I was ecstatic, and I could only pray it stayed this way.

When that song went off, "Midnight Snack" by Muni Long came on. It gave me all the nineties R&B vibes that I felt when I was with my man. I held on to the steering wheel tightly as I sang along.

Walked in the door
Sace on the floor
Do it again like you did it before
Bed or the floor
I'll take either or
I get mine then you get yours
But I'm not keeping score
It's me on you
And you on me
And that's the way that it should be
I like when we do what we do
Started out at midnight and now it's quarter to two

Meet me in the kitchen for a midnight snack
Keep my body on your coming back-to-back
Right, right now don't keep me waiting
Need it now ASAP
Meet me in the kitchen for a midnight snack

By the time I had pulled up to the tall building in front of me, I had performed a whole concert. I texted Broderick to let him know I was here. The area looked nice, but there was no way I was exiting this car without him coming to get me. He let me know he was coming, so I gathered my purse and my charger to be ready.

When Broderick got to my door, he opened it and lifted me out of the car effortlessly. He was looking far more fresh and clean than he had this morning. He was wearing a gray Nike sweatsuit with some J's and no coat on. When my feet touched the ground, I almost didn't want to walk. I wanted him to carry me the whole way into the building.

"I missed you," he said, while he caressed my behind mid-air.

"I missed you, too, king," I retorted with a smile on my face.

"Whose care is this?" He looked at me, puzzled.

"Mine," I shrugged. "You paid for the deposit." I winked. "Now, where are we?" I asked once he put me down.

"Good, girl," he complimented me. "Listen, don't nobody know about this spot but you so you can't say shit," he warned.

"I already sent someone my location," I shrugged, sheepishly.

"What? Who? It better not be that light skinned chick you've been hanging out with!" He frowned.

"No." I was confused. "Just my sister; now, what's your issue with Kecia?"

"I don't trust her," he stated blankly.

My head jerked back. "Did she do something I need to know about?"

"She hasn't done anything to prove she's to be trusted," he flicked his nostrils. "Anyway, this is me, J, and LJ's crib. Each of us has a floor."

"What? What made y'all move all the way to no man's land?" I wondered.

"Because no one knows us out here. Come on," he said. He took me to the second floor, which was his. Apparently Jason lived on the first floor. When he opened the door to his apartment, I instantly started looking around at any and everything. It was nicely decorated and very clean, but it lacked color. Everything was gray and bland.

"Hmm..." I said as I examined the Cloud sofa he had gotten from RH. I knew because I loved that couch when I shopped there.

"You don't like it?" He stood back, awaiting my assessment. I eyed him, confused. Why would I express disdain for *his* home? "The place. You don't like it?"

I shrugged. "It's cute. I'd add just a little more color. Like, either beige or white. Everything is so monochromatic, but it looks nice." I paused to think for a minute. "You just need a hint of a woman's touch, and it would be perfect.

"Mmm hmm..." he said as he got behind me and circled his arms around my waist. "Is that right?"

"Yeah," I confirmed. "You see how you don't have no pictures in here or nothing? You need family photos or some of you and your frat or something."

Broderick's place was very spacious. He had a very nice two-bedroom apartment, only one of which he used as an actual room. The other was a closet. The closet held ever pair of Jordan ever made. I was astounded by how many pairs of Timberlands this man owned. The all looked the same to me, but according to him, they were completely different, and once one pair creased, he had to get another one. Literally, insane.

"Speaking of family, me and my grandfather had words. I went to find you and talk to you about it, but that's when your neighbor told me you'd moved out."

"Well, why did y'all get into it?" I inquired, while picking a piece of lint from his sweatshirt.

Broderick sighed and directed me to have a seat on

the couch. He told me all about the dude, Red—who I was familiar with from playing with the Bulls— and his coach encouraging him to play professional sports. I was stunned by how much had gone on in his life without me.

"So, what do you think?" he asked.

I blew out a gust of wind. "I think if you don't sign up for the draft, you're crazier than I thought."

Broderick released a guffaw laughing at me. "Nigga, what?"

"Yes! Like, if it's not God's will, you won't get in; but you're telling me that you don't want to be the star athlete that you naturally are because you have a dream to be a nefarious clown?" I eyed him quizzically. "Make it make sense, babe. Your granddaddy was right, and so was Red."

He waved me off. "But them players don't make no real money, the owners do."

"Then, nigga, play 'til you can buy a team. The heck?" I was confused. "What's the real reason why you don't want to sign up for the draft?"

He shrugged. "I've never had to *apply* or be considered for nothing in this world. Things always come easily to me. My last name has merit."

"So, you have a problem with trying because you're afraid of possible rejection...and authority," I hypothesized.

"I didn't say I had a problem with authority—"

"Nah, that wasn't a question. You do." I cut him off.

Broderick picked me up in the air, then slammed me back down unto the coach, sending me into a tickling fit.

"Staaaaahp!" I cried out, laughing.

"Okay; okay," he finally calmed down.

After I finally caught my breath, I said, "If you don't call them and tell them you want to be considered for the draft, I'm breaking up with you. Stop being weird. They can't reject what they need. The team needs you."

Broderick looked at me like I had grown two heads. "Let me take you out on a date before somebody tries to come and snatch you up."

I chuckled. "That's the least of your worries. Besides, I'm all yours." I found my way into his lap and straddled him. "Thank you for wanting to take me out, but I'm in the mood to stay in. I just want to read a book and sip on some wine while you rub my booty and watch the game. That's all I need."

Broderick adjusted me so I could sit right on his strong man. "Coming right up." He flashed his megawatt smile before kissing me.

"Oh, and Broderick," I said into his mouth.

"Hmm?"

"I wasn't going nowhere with you in them hoe pants."

His head jerked back in stun.

"Nigga, all I see is print and possibilities. Burn all them up, and I'm not playing." I folded my arms across my chest.

"Yes, ma'am. Whatever makes you happy, dear." We both fell out laughing and prepared for our night in.

I got up and walked to his room.

"Can I get one of your t-shirts?" I requested. I was trying to get comfortable today. I wanted to rock Broderick's favorite attire. A tee and panties. I'd add some socks because his place was a bit cold for my liking.

My love eyed me with his crooked smile. "What're you trying to do, girl?"

I shrugged. "I'm just trying to get comfortable," I played coy.

"Mmm hmm..." He toyed with the wiry hairs on his chin. "Top drawer."

"Thanks," I said. I ambled over to the dresser and took the remote and handed it to my man. "The game is on."

Without waiting on him to turn on the television, I turned around and stripped right out of my clothes. I was down to the ankle socks, bra, and panties.

"Sky..."

"Turn the game on, babe," I uttered and kept undressing. The bra was killing my vibe. I took it off and stuffed it in my purse with the rest of my clothes and retrieved my book.

I put the t-shirt on, which fell in the right place. It was too big for me, but it left the bottoms of my cheeks out with the cheeky underwear I had on. I felt like I looked the prettiest in this state.

I turned to find my man staring at me hungrily. "What?" I asked in a kittenish tone.

He cleared his throat and said, "I'm trying to be a gentleman." with his right brow elevated.

"Then be a gentleman." I quipped.

I extended my right hand to the bed. I was inviting this man into his own bed so we can have an intimate moment. Not necessarily sexual, just intimate. Just us. Broderick eyed me quizzically, then complied. He stripped down to the boxers, finally turned on the television, and joined me in his high-rise California king. He laid with his back pressed up against his pillows and I made myself comfortable in his arms. With each of his toned legs on either side and his arms around my waist, I felt so loved.

Boy, I know you can't help but to be yourself 'round me
Yourself 'round me, now
And I know nobody's perfect, so I'll let you be, I'll let you be
It's the way you wear your emotions on both of your sleeves,
ah-ah-ah
To the face you make when I tell you that I have to leave,
ooh-ooh

But I like it, baby, ooh, I like it, baby
But I like it, baby, baby, but I like it, baby
Ah, we don't need the world's acceptance
They're too hard on me, they're too hard on you, boy
I'll always be your secret weapon in your arsenal, your
arsenal
And I know you had it rough growing up, but that's okay
(that's okay)
I like it rough (that's okay, baby)
Even when you let your feelings get in the way (let your
feelings get in the way)

I was laying on my side, reading this book for the second time, yet I felt every single emotion I had the first go around. The fact that Chance's gargantuan hand was massaging my ass and back didn't make it any better. I also had my Raycon's in my ears, playing Beyoncé's "Plastic Off The Sofa".

I still like it, baby, ooh, I like it, baby (like it, baby)
But I like it, baby (like it, baby)
Baby, baby (like it, baby)
I still like it, baby, baby, baby, baby
Say, say you won't change
I love the little things that make you, you
Ooh, the rest of the world is strange
Stay in our lane, just you and me, and our family

I think you're so cool (even though I'm cooler than you)
Boy, I love that you can't help but be yourself around me
Yourself around me
Sugar, well you're trippin', I know we'll make up and
make love
So I'll let you be, I'll let you be
It's the way you listen when I'm cryin'
You let me lean in
It's the way you want one more kiss after you said you were
leavin'

Apparently, I was emoting a little too much to the material because he suddenly muted the television and said, "What the hell is in that book that's good your breath hitching and you stirring all in my lap?"

I giggled and flipped over to my stomach and took the ear buds out. "Baby, Pastor Ezra is wild. He's my latest book bae!"

Chance waved me off. "A pastor? Nigga, please."

"Uh huuuuh!" I handed him the book.

But I like it, baby (yes, I like it, baby, yes, I like it baby)
Yes, I like it, baby (like it, baby)
Like it, I like it, I love it, baby
I like it, baby
I like it, I love it, baby
I like it, baby (I like it, ooh, like it, I like it, yeah)

I like, like it, baby
I like it, baby
Oh, I like it, baby
Baby, come on over (ooh, I like it, baby)
And I need you, baby
Baby (na-na-na, na-na-na, na-na, na-na)

"Ezra peppered my belly with wet kisses between the ropes. And shit! It felt like blissful teasing in between the restricted sections of my flesh. I turned my head and focused on his long leg that was spread out aside me. He even looked damn good in dress shoes. When his mouth made its way below my belly button my spine jolted, but Ezra didn't slow." Broderick turned his nose up at me while reading the passage aloud. "I thought you was saved! Is that what you freaky ass church people do?"

I playfully popped him in the chest. "I didn't get freaky for real until I met yo' heathen ass." I stuck my tongue out at him.

Broderick leaned down and caught it in his mouth. He palmed my behind aggressively, then pulled me up to straddle him.

"You bet not've been freaking with nobody but me." He tongued my neck, knowing that was my weakness. My nipples pebbled and I was reduced to a waterfall almost immediately.

Without warning, Broderick removed his hands from my heated body. I saw him grab my book.

"What are you doing?" I panted, as he read a little more of the excerpt.

He ignored my question. "Sing me a song." His request was muffled inside the groove of my neck.

"Huh?" I asked, caught up in the euphoric feeling of my baby's tongue painting my neck with lust.

He spanked my ass and bit down on my neck. "Sing me a song."

"What do you want to hear?" I groaned. I was like puddy in this man's hands.

"Anything." His head lowered to my left boob. He lifted his shirt and put the whole thing in his mouth, then released it with a popping sound. "Sing about me." He shrugged.

"Aiight," I squirmed, trying to focus on the H.E.R.'s lyrics.

Baby, the sound of you
Better than a harmony
I want you off my mind
And on me
Holding me closer than we've ever been before
This ain't a dream
You're here with me
Boy, it don't get no better than you

For you, I wanna take my time
All night
I wanna love you in every kind of way
I wanna please you, no matter how long it takes
If the world should end tomorrow and we only have today
I'm gonna love you in every kind of way

I felt him pull my underwear to the side, and my hips formed an 's'. I couldn't focus on the song anymore. I inquired for the last time, "What are you doing?"

"I'm following the pastor's lead," he sighed as we became one. I couldn't tell where he began or where I ended. Just Black skin everywhere. We were our ancestors' wet dreams, basking in the light of the sun, drowning in the sea of infinity, dancing to the rhythm of love's drum. "I'm your book bae, now." Broderick toss my book off the bed and sent me into a frenzy.

Chapter Twelve

SKYLAR

Broderick and I had officially been in complete bliss for the past two months. I was finally thinking about just moving forward and telling my family that we were together. I mean, since neither he nor I saw ourselves with anyone else, we should just go ahead and live out loud. Consequences be damned.

In the meantime, though, I declined moving in with him. It was way too soon for me to be moving out of my parents' house after telling them I needed to come back home. Plus, it left room for us to actually miss one another. Broderick and I had been dating like two regular college kids, and I loved it. I wish we could've had this from the beginning with no breaks, but we were here now and that's all that mattered.

"How are things going with the baby? I know he's almost ready to get up out of there," I danced in my seat nervously. I asked because I cared. It was the humane thing to do. Nicole was having a difficult pregnancy, and although I did not like her at all, I would not wish that on my worst enemy. Truthfully, he'd done a great job of keeping us in our separate corners, which bought me time to come to grips with the fact that they were both going to be in the picture.

"He's coming along. Nicole's blood pressure was extremely high again at the last visit so she's on bed rest," he stated.

I nodded my head, awkwardly. "I'm praying for the baby. I hope he has a safe delivery."

We were tucked away in a corner at Eddie V's, a very nice restaurant in downtown Chicago. Nothing on the menu was less than fifty big ones. Most of the people in here were older than us, but we were in our element. The both of us looked amazing. I donned a white, turtleneck bodysuit that hugged my small boobs to perfection. I paired it with some high waisted, white bellbottoms, a tan Gucci bag, and clear heels. And I threw on a cream, faux fur coat to top it off. My makeup look was neutral. I had celebrity makeup artist, Jazzmin, beat my face. She was known for doing makeup for the beauty influencers, like Ari. I felt like I was in the third heaven being here. Broderick smelled and looked like a million bucks. I was finally able to get this fool to dress up. He was matching my fly in a white turtleneck, chocolate, cropped cigar trousers and chocolate oxfords. He looked like the boss he was destined to become, and I looked like the kept woman I wanted to be. We were celebrating. His request for an evaluation by the NBA Undergraduate Advisory Committee was submitted in writing two days after the NCAA tournament concluded; Broderick had been assessed by the committee, which included executives from twenty NBA teams. My man was looking good on the courts and people were starting to take notice. Soon he'd be heading to the draft combine to show off his skills for the higher ups. I believed he would soon be rocking a Bulls jersey with the number sixteen on it. I couldn't wait.

"By the way, you look delicious, Mr. Sinclair," I winked, flirting with my man.

"Ah man," he blushed. "Nah, a nigga had to step up his game. I'm at a table with a star." He winked at me. "How were classes today?"

"Fine," I shrugged, while taking a sip of my lemonade. We had already placed our order for appetizers, and I couldn't wait for them to arrive. I was starving. "Classes have been fine. I've just been so tired. I need to just take a day to catch up on sleep because my sleep schedule's been off."

"Mmm..." he nodded. "Well, I brought you here just so we can spend some alone time together. We've been kicking it inside, but today I wanted to show off my girl. I don't know how many more Netflix movies I can take," he jested.

I chuckled. "Well, it does feel good to be outside with the man that I love."

"Ditto, shawty. Like, I don't know how or when, but you've become a part of me. I don't work without you." Broderick bit his lip. "It, low key, scares me, but it's you for me. Whenever I go through something or have good news, I don't even think to call my brother or anyone else first. You're who I want to talk to. That is wild to me."

"Okay, lady and gentleman," our waiter placed my plate in front of me. "Here are your lobster tacos; and here are your crab cakes, sir."

"Thank you," we said in unison. "Will there be anything else while we get these entrees going for you?"

I shook my head at Broderick, and he offered the verbal 'no, thank you.'

"Now, back to our conversation," Broderick said, while cutting into his crab cake.

"Hold on," I said, then closed my eyes and offered a

silent prayer. When I opened them, Broderick's eyes were on mine.

"Let me ask you something," Broderick changed the subject.

"Shoot."

"What do you be saying when you close your eyes and pray?"

I eyed him, wondering where this inquiry was coming from all of a sudden. Broderick had never asked me about prayer before. From what he had told me, he barely recognized God as real.

"Um..." I thought about it. "I start with acknowledging God for being God, then I express thanksgiving, then I make a request." I shrugged. "I guess that's about it."

Broderick nodded his head up and down while taking a bit of his crab cake into his mouth. "You think I can do that with you sometimes?"

"What? Pray?" I quizzed.

He shrugged. "Yeah, I mean, you and Red do it all the time. Maybe I need to do it with you."

I placed my fork down and beckoned for his hands. My heart was beaming, radiating on the inside. My man was slowly but surely being introduced to my God. "I can teach you a prayer now, if you'd like."

"As long as it ain't one of them long ones you be

doing at night. I don't need my damn food getting cold, ma," his face folded.

"Hush," I giggled. "Just close your eyes and repeat after me, 'Our Father which art in heaven, hallowed be thy name. Thy kingdom come, thy will be done on earth, as it is in heaven. Give us this day our daily bread. And forgive us our debts, as we forgive our debtors. And lead us not into temptation but deliver us from evil: For thine is the kingdom, and the power, and the glory, forever. Amen.'"

Broderick recited each line perfectly. "What did all that mean?"

I fanned myself, being so moved by his journey. "It meant that you acknowledge God for being our heavenly Father. You then ask for His will to be done in your life. You asked if He would forgive your sins as you learn to forgive others; and that all power belongs to God."

He nodded his head while continuing to stuff his face.

"So, the draft," I wiggled in my seat. "It's coming soon!"

Broderick nodded. "Indeed, it is."

"You excited?" Shoot, I was excited enough to celebrate though nothing was solidified yet. "You took a leap of faith. That *has* to be exciting." I took a bite of my taco. As soon as the flavors hit my pallet, I danced in my seat and rubbed my tummy. I had to bite it carefully to ensure that the food did not disrupt my lip gloss or stain my top. I had to be cute all night.

"That good, huh?" he eyed me. I stopped squirming immediately, feeling self-conscious. "You don't have to be shy. I love it when you eat."

I smirked, "What? That's crazy."

"Nah, 'cause your little ass can put away some food, and it cracks me up." He shrugged.

"You literally like the craziest things about me and it's weird," I laughed hardily.

Broderick shrugged. "I mean, I love the simple things: you in a bonnet and my t-shirt just reading to me, you cursing me out, the way your pupils dilate when you're trying to decide whether you want to flip on the crazy switch in your mind or if you want to stay sane—"

"Boy, what?" I laughed even harder. My entire frame shook as I tried to get control of my diaphragm. "Who says that?"

He shrugged. "I like 'em a little crazy."

I shook my head. "*That's* what you love about me? That's why you love me?"

He shook his head. "Nah, that ain't the why, though that is what attracted me to you initially."

I tilted my head to the left, intrigued. "Well, I know that you love me. I can feel that you love me. Why do you love me?"

My love cleared his throat and reached across the

table to hold my hands. He blew out a deep breath and paused. "It's a simple question, but it ain't a simple answer." He took another breath. His wind smelled of peppermint oils and honey. Those chocolate pools called his eyes carried so much pain yet so much purpose. I got lost in them each time. I could sit and admire him all day long. "Uh... it's because of how you love me."

I blushed.

"It's a very spiritual love," he teared up, which shocked me. "Like, it goes beyond my comprehension. I've been through a lot, but you've never seen me for what I've been through, you know? You see me for the best that I can give to the world, or to my family and friends."

I reached over and thumbed away one of his tears he let slip.

"When everything starts to weigh on me, you breathe life back into me. That's why I love you. I love you because you're you. I love you because you're you to me."

"Baby," I whimpered, joining him with tears of happiness.

"You're a joy that I get to experience in this life until I don't anymore," he continued. "Until I meet you in the air or in the next life. However God does it." He pressed my hands to the left side of his chest. "I don't really know His methods, but if He's as good as you say He is, He's got to let me see you in the by and by."

I nodded, again. I was so speechless and overwhelmed by his affection towards me. My nigga was a street nigga. He only had softness for me. Everyone else got a rock. He only showed his emotions to me. And I counted it as a privilege.

"This is God engineered so it's perfect. Whatever obstacles I got to go through to get to you, I'll go through them, because that's how God shows me His love – through you, Skylar. That's why I love you. Because God loves me."

I bowed my and let the tears fall from my eyes. "Thank you for loving me." I wiped my eyes. "I count it an honor that you would think enough of me to be vulnerable, to share your innermost thoughts with me." I sniffled. "Black men don't have safe spaces. Y'all carry so much on a day-to-day basis just for being born and being Black. Just by the nature of our experience in this country, y'all don't even get a chance to smile before you weep. It's a life of pressure, depression, and oppression. Post traumatic slave syndrome being passed down the generational pipeline through the bloodstream like a disease—because it is one. We see niggas being executed on social media like it's nothing. We march for our niggas; fight for our niggas; fight with our niggas; and even have to deal with the pain inflicted by the same niggas we love when they turn around and oppress us."

"But when you find a nigga than honors you enough to know that the sun rises and falls around you. One who will turn on the blinders to every woman but you. One who is trying to better himself in a world that tells him better is unavailable. When the nigga becomes a king and lays his head in your bosom, you don't snatch the crown and make him a jester." I wiped my eyes. "You make the kingdom a safe place." I nodded. "Your emotions are safe with me; I won't use them against you. And I'm in love with you."

Broderick coolly stood from his seat and sauntered over to mine. With his large, possessive hand, he put it around my throat. He did not care that we were in a restaurant full of people. I didn't either. None of them mattered. We were in our own little corner, in our own little world. Broderick bent down and nibbled on my bottom lip lightly before taking my whole mouth in his. This kiss was so nasty and other worldly that we might go to jail for indecent exposure, though we were still clothed. Our tongues smacked together like the sounds of lightning in the night's sky. Apparently, some people were watching because we heard cheering behind us. I didn't know how long the lip-lock lasted, but I knew I had to be in love because I didn't even trip off him choking me with his nasty little hand on my white top.

Finally, he pulled back a little.

"Can you give me a napkin?" I tried to cover my face, but he used his other hand to smack my hand away while the right one was still around my neck.

"What're you covering your face for? You ashamed of my love?" he smirked.

"No, sir," I said firmly. "I think I have a visitor in my nose." I wiggled my nose around.

"Which nostril?"

I pointed to my right. And with all the insanity he could muster up, this negro dug his left pinky into my nose and pulled out the booger. I secretly hoped no one saw what he did as he wiped it on a napkin. But I was just as weird as he was because that made me love him even more.

"Aye, me pay the bill and let's go home," he said suggestively.

Before I could even answer him, I heard, "STOP! STEVIE, STOOOOOP!"

The very next thing I could hear was dishes clasping together. Our table was ripped from in front of us as I witnessed my brother charging towards us like a raging bull, while a very pregnant Tajma waddled behind him, trying to stop him.

"Ah!" I screamed, and instantly got into the fetal position to protect myself.

"Imma beat yo' mutha..." Lil Steve didn't even finish

the sentence. His fist descended into Broderick's jaw with a vengeance. All in this nice establishment. He had lost his mind. I was stunned to the core that my man wasn't fighting back.

"Lil Steve, stop!" I screamed.

Hit after hit, Lil Steve tagged Broderick, who was now on the floor.

"Bae!" Tajma yelled.

"Somebody call the police!"

Within seconds, chaos had ensued. The patrons had gone from cheering for us to calling the po-pos on us. I was so embarrassed. So humiliated. So hurt.

"I told you... to... look out... for her... and you take advantage of her?" Lil Steve said in between punches.

"I love her, nigga!" Broderick finally spoke up.

"I will..." Broderick said through gritted teeth. He popped Broderick in the mouth like his name was Nipsey Hussle. "I had you around my family and you do this?"

"Lil Steve, stop!" I yelled. I ran over to them, physically trying to pry my brother's brawny frame from the love of my life. "The police are coming."

"Stay out of this, Skylar!" he yelled over his shoulder at me. "This treacherous nigga knows what he did!"

"Bae, let's go NOW!" Tajma hollered as we heard sirens.

Lil Steve finally got off Chance. He was tired and out

of breath. The look in his eye was so vicious that it terrified me. "Let's go, Sky!" My brother bid for me by grabbing on my arm and pulling me towards the door.

"No!" I yelled while snatching away from him. I ran over to Broderick and kneeled before him. "Baby, are you okay?" His mouth was so bloody, and he had bruises all over his face. I was horrified.

"You seriously taking this nigga side over your own blood?" Lil Steve got in my face.

"He didn't do anything wrong! You just came in here losing your shit because you saw us together. But it's really not your business." I cried.

"It *is* my business!" He gritted. "Why you think this nigga's quiet and eating this shit? I tell this nigga that you can be gullible and that niggas take advantage of you and the next thing we know he's sniffing up behind you?"

"What's going on over here?" Chicago's finest and the managers had walked right in on our moment.

Tajma began talking to the police. It was likely that my brother was going to jail for losing his shit. But could what Lil Steve just said be true? Did Chance prey on me because he felt like I was an easy target or was what I felt real. Tears flooded my eyes as I turned to look at Chance.

"Did you—"

"What we have is real," he stated while trying to

check on his busted lip. "I ain't even think about that shit. I'm in love with you!"

Lil Steve took off again in his direction.

"Hey, stop!" Tajma yelled.

"You're under arrest!" I heard the police yell while trying to get ahold of him.

"Oh my God!" I heard the patrons shouting as the police dragged my brother out of the establishment. I was so embarrassed and so hurt.

"Where are y'all taking him?" Tajma yelled to twelve.

"Twenty-sixth and California, ma'am," the officer yelled over his shoulder while stuffing the bull that was my brother into the squad car. "I need somebody to take me to my fiancé!"

I was stunned into silence. This is not quite how I wanted to tell my brother—or anyone for that matter. Apparently he and Tajma were on a date, and seeing us together triggered his insanity.

"I'll take you," Chance said. He needed some medical attention for his lip. Lil Steve had wilded out on his face. I couldn't believe him. "I'll call Jason so he can get him out. I know Lil Steve ain't trying to see me right now." He moped.

"Good idea. Let's go," Tajma waddled to the doorway.

Chance found the waiter and gave him some bills for our food. Lil Steve had ruined the entire day for me.

Now the clock was racing. I could no longer keep our love a secret. Now, it was only a matter of time before word would begin to spread, so I had to break the news to everyone today—before anyone else could.

Chance stopped us before we could go outside. He looked me dead in my eyes and said, "You're my world. It's me and you period, until the wheels fall off. I wasn't trying to fight your brother because he is my brother, my superior in the organization. Well, he was when he was an active member. I should have never dated you. I knew this day would come when he would feel betrayed, but you can't help who you fall in love with. And I'm in love with you. For real and for the right reasons. You believe me? Please, tell me you believe me."

I pondered for a quick second, then nodded my head. You can't fake chemistry this real. I didn't think my brother was lying, but I also don't think he had all the facts. He didn't know about our love. He only understood his own feelings.

Hand in hand, we walked out of the restaurant toward his car with Tajma. We had about an eighteen-minute ride from the restaurant that Lil Steve tore up to the precinct.

When we got in, Tajma started crying. "I tried to stop him, y'all. He just don't listen. Lil' Steve just does not listen. When he gets mad, he's like a raging bull."

"I know," I whispered and reached back and rubbed

her hand.

Broderick hadn't uttered a word. His phone began to light up and ring though. The name *Nicole* flashed across the screen. He looked down and then back at me. I shook my head. This day was clearly not getting any better for me.

"Answer it for me. She might've gone into labor," he stated.

I guess if he could take the blows from my rock-headed brother, I could play nice for his baby mama.

"Hello?" I answered, and quickly put the phone on speaker.

The pause was pregnant. "Who is this?"

I looked around, confused. "Skylar, who else?" Because I was trying to figure out how many other women did she think would be answering his phone.

"Oh you!" She pretended to be shocked. "Where's daddy at?"

She was officially playing with me right now, and I would have thought she would have learned the lesson after the last time.

"Oop," Tajma said in the back.

"Aye, chill," Broderick interjected. "What do you need?"

"I'm just calling to see what you were doing," she said in a pseudo-vixen voice.

"He's busy being in this kitty is what he's doing.

What about you, trashy?" All the consideration I had for her went out of the window since she wanted to play with the kid.

Tajma couldn't even hold her laughter inside anymore. She held her belly and chuckled to the high heavens. "Oh, God!" She wiped the tears from her eyes.

Chance gave me a look that pleaded for me to stop, but it was too late.

"Oh, that ole thing?" Nicole asked with much venom in her voice. "You talking about the same kitty that you got his first baby vacuumed out of? Or did you get a new kitty since the abortion?"

Every bit of air escaped from my lungs immediately. So many questions filled my head. *How did she know my deepest, darkest sin? Who told her? Did she get this information from Kecia? How could God allow this to happen?* My eyes grew wide as saucers. The cat had gotten my tongue. The hag had won. The fat lady had begun to sing. I was sinking.

"I—" before I could even respond.

"What the—" was the last thing I heard Broderick say before hearing the tires screeching on the road.

**THE END.
TO BE CONTINUED IN "THE
COMMENCEMENT".**

Thank you!

Thank you for reading! Please, leave a review on Amazon!

Also by Sheridan S. Davis

Saved Sex

Pretty For A Dark-Skin Girl

I'm Nobody's Ruth

Church Girls

Church Girls 2

With Love

Church Girls 3

Church Girls 4

Blood Diamond: Diamond In A Rough

Blood Diamond: Diamond Dust

Blood Diamond: 24K

Untitled: How Does It Feel

Another Sad Love Song

Late Registration

Made in the USA
Monee, IL
23 April 2024

57338883R00164